THE
WHISPERING
MUSE

THE
WHISPERING
MUSE

THE
WHISPERING
MUSE

SJÓN

TRANSLATED FROM THE ICELANDIC BY VICTORIA CRIBB

FARRAR, STRAUS AND GIROUX   NEW YORK

Farrar, Straus and Giroux
18 West 18th Street, New York 10011

Printed in the United States of America
Originally published in Icelandic in 2005 by Bjartur, Iceland, as
Argóarflísin
English translation originally published in 2012 by Telegram,
Great Britain
Published in the United States by Farrar, Straus and Giroux
First American edition, 2013

Library of Congress Cataloging-in-Publication Data
Sjón, 1962–
    [Argóarflísin. English]
    The whispering muse / Sjón ; translated from the Icelandic by
Victoria Cribb.
        p.   cm.
    American edition of the English translation originally published
in 2012 by Telegram, Great Britain.
    ISBN 978-0-374-28907-2 (alk. paper)
    1. Caeneus (Greek mythology)—Fiction.   2. Sea stories—
Fiction.   I. Cribb, Victoria.   II. Title.

PT7511.S62 A7413 2012b
839'.6935—dc23

                                                    2012038900

Designed by Jonathan D. Lippincott

www.fsgbooks.com
www.twitter.com/fsgbooks • www.facebook.com/fsgbooks

10   9   8   7   6   5   4   3   2   1

On the celestial charts of the scientific treatise *Almagest*, written in the mid-second century by the cosmologist Claudius Ptolemy, there was a vast constellation called Argo Navis (The Ship *Argo*), named for Jason son of Aeson's galley of many nails. This assembly of stars could not be seen until one reached Alexandria by night, but from there the *Argo* was clearly visible traversing the southern skies with all oars out and bellying sail, voyaging into the unknown in search of the Golden Fleece—while around her floated the lesser constellations, Centaurus (The Centaur) and Hydra (The Sea Monster).

Sixteen centuries later, Earth was no longer at the center of the universe and men set about drawing themselves a new heaven. It was then that the French astronomer Nicolas Louis de Lacaille decided that the Argo Navis was far too large and unwieldy, so he dismantled the ship, retaining some parts and jettisoning others, and created, in the process, three new constellations:

Carina (The Keel), Puppis (The Poop), and Vela (The Sail).

But we old-timers say:
—She sails there still!

—from "Seven Ships"
by Capt. Hans Caron Alfredson

BACKGROUND
TO THE VOYAGE

I

I, Valdimar Haraldsson, was in my twenty-seventh year
when I embarked on the publication of a small journal
devoted to my chief preoccupation, the link between fish
consumption and the superiority of the Nordic race. It
was written in Danish, under the title *Fisk og Kultur*, and
came out in seventeen volumes over the space of twenty
years. During the First World War, publication was suspended for two years—and the sixth and seventh volumes were only half complete, i.e., only two issues each,
as fate decreed that following the death of my first wife
I was confined to my bed for eight months, from late Au-
gust 1910 until spring 1911. Then the extent of the read-
ers' loyalty to the periodical was revealed, as I see from
my records that the only parties who canceled their sub-
scriptions were the University of Kraków and the Kjós
Parish Reading Society. I won't go further into the rea-
sons here but will refer anyone who may be interested to
my book *Memoirs of a Herring Inspector* (pub. Fisk og
Kultur, Copenhagen, 1933).

The content of the journal was written primarily in

foreign tongues, as I knew that the majority of my ideas would be far too newfangled for my countrymen, indeed would pass way over their heads. For they hadn't even heard of the recent scientific advances on which I based my theory, which was reiterated on the title page of every issue:

> It is our belief that the Nordic race, which has fished off the maritime coast for countless generations and thus enjoyed a staple diet of seafood, owes its physical and intellectual prowess above all to this type of nutrition, and that the Nordic race is for this reason superior in vigor and attainments to other races that have not enjoyed such ease of access to the riches of the ocean.

The final issue of each volume included a summary of the year's best articles and essays, translated into Hungarian by my brother-in-law, the psychiatrist Dr. György Pázmány. Every issue also included bits and bobs to fill up the pages, chiefly droll stories and occasional verses from my childhood home in the county of Kjós, all in Icelandic, which I left untranslated.

As one might expect, I was for a long time the sole author of the scientific articles in *Fisk og Kultur*, but as the journal gained a wider circulation I received ever greater numbers of letters and contributions from foreign enthusiasts on these topics. While most were interested in fish consumption, there were also quite a few devotees of Nordic racial history. However, it was a rare man who perceived—as I, the editor, did—how inextricably these two factors were linked. Primus inter pares among the latter group was the Danish ship broker Hermann Jung-Olsen, then hardly out of his teenage years yet already showing an unusual brilliance of mind. He was one of those individuals who inspire benevolence and sympathy from the very first encounter, deepening on more intimate acquaintance into respect and trust. For Hermann Jung-Olsen was a fine figure of a man, a firebrand with an insatiable appetite for work. He was born with a silver spoon in his mouth, yet although his childhood home was one of the most elegant in Copenhagen, there was fish on the table at least four times a week, not only on weekdays but on high days and holidays too. This was mainly because his father, Magnus Jung-Olsen, was of the old school when it came to money—a strict man who never rushed into anything or did a precipitate deed in his life, a great man indeed.

The reason for my bringing up the publishing history of *Fisk og Kultur* here is that a whole eight years after the appearance of the final issue I received a letter from the great ship operator, the aforementioned Magnus Jung-Olsen, father of my late young friend Hermann, in which he invited me on a cruise with the MS *Elizabet Jung-Olsen*, a merchant vessel of the Kronos line, the Jung-Olsen family firm. Recently launched, she was due to embark on her maiden voyage, conveying raw paper from Norway to Izmit in Turkey and continuing from there to Poti in Soviet Georgia to pick up a cargo of tea that the locals cultivate on the Kolkheti coastal plain and prepare for export in the exemplary tea factories provided for them by Stalin.

Mr. Jung-Olsen says in his letter that his son long dreamed of doing me some sort of favor—as he had mentioned more than once—and that the old shipping magnate had been reminded of this fact when he received my telegram of condolence on the anniversary of Hermann's death, nearly four years after his untimely end (he was murdered on the day peace was declared, in a *Bierkeller* brawl in Vienna).

The letter reached me at the end of March, at a time when I had long been in low spirits (my second wife having passed away that very month the previous year), but now my heart was filled with unfeigned joy: joy at being invited on such an adventure; joy that one could still meet with such charity from one man to another; joy that the buds looked promising on the boughs of the apple trees in the tiny patch of garden that belonged to my foolish neighbor Widow Lauritzen, although the poor neglected creatures had suffered cruelly in the February storms. Yes, such was my joy when I read Mr. Magnus Jung-Olsen's letter.

And I read it often.

In 1908 I published a witty anecdote in the spring

issue of *Fisk og Kultur*. For some reason it popped into my mind as I stood there at the kitchen window in Copenhagen, the letter still clutched in my hand:

Once there were two gentlemen who met in a park while out walking their dogs. The younger instantly doffed his hat to the elder, who nodded in acknowledgment. Then, as chance would have it, the younger man's dog tore itself loose and raced off after a squirrel. The young man was embarrassed and started apologizing to the elder, saying that his dog had never done this sort of thing before; he had no business frightening squirrels; this was a one-off; it wouldn't happen again, he could promise that.

The elder gentleman listened patiently to his apologies, then putting his head on one side, said with a twinkle in his eye:

"Young man, is it possible that you are confusing me with little Mr. Esquirol?"

Dr. Pázmány and I were so tickled by this story that we added it to the Hungarian summary that year.

But I doubt my countrymen would have made head or tail of it.

LIFE ON
THE OCEAN WAVE

II

At eleven o'clock on the morning of April 10, 1949, the merchant ship MS *Elizabet Jung-Olsen* departed the free port of Copenhagen en route to Norway, bound for Mold Bay in the county of Vest-Agder. My quarters on board consisted of two spacious cabins amidships on the port side below the bridge, the outer room entered from the saloon. This cabin contained every conceivable comfort: a berth and chairs, desk, cupboards, and bookshelves, all as neatly made as one could wish for. The inner cabin consisted of a bathroom with a china washbasin, a mirror as long as the space permitted, and a deep bathtub on bronze feet shaped like the claws of a dragon or lion (one can't always tell them apart). Opening off the bathroom was a roomy closet containing a modern WC. I couldn't help thinking that it would be interesting to see the captain's quarters, given the comfort of the accommodation afforded to the "supernumeraries," as they call those who are over and above the crew.

Well, I was now extremely glad that I had dropped by at my benefactor's headquarters on my way to the ship that morning to deliver a letter of thanks. I had worked on its composition far into the night, making three drafts before the final clean copy, for in addition to conveying my gratitude, I wished heartily to congratulate Mr. Magnus Jung-Olsen on the success of his remarkable company.

I sat down by the porthole and looked out over the sound. The sky was overcast, a stiff northerly breeze sending a considerable swell head-on to the ship. The whistle blew from time to time, at lengthy intervals. Ahead nothing could be seen but the crests of the waves, slapping their white foam hither and thither as they swelled and subsided in turn. Sleet began to pelt from the sky and the view faded. I watched until I could no longer distinguish sky from sea, then lay down, worn out from my letter-writing the night before.

I set my alarm clock for five p.m. The food on board the vessels of the Kronos line is famed throughout the shipping world and it is claimed that the Danish king borrows their chefs when His Majesty's own ship's cook is indisposed.

•

I was shown to a seat at the captain's table, where Captain Alfredson introduced me to the first and second mates, the first engineer, and the purser. There was a woman there too, the purser's wife, I assumed, but later gathered that their marital status was somewhat irregular and it would be more correct to call her his lady friend. Apparently I was not to be the only supernumerary on this trip.

The woman, who had thick fair hair, was of below average height and stoutly built. She seemed half afraid of me, or at least inordinately shy. I thought she was goggling at me but later observed that this expression was habitual, for on closer acquaintance I noticed that in addition to large eyes set rather low in her face, she had a drooping lower lip that caused her to gape inadvertently between sentences. She was German or, by her own account, Polish by family and birth, or even Lithuanian, but apparently spoke German to her gentleman friend. She understood a little Danish but didn't speak it, as the couple had only been together three seasons. At this stage it didn't occur to me to delve any further into her situation or life story, as I assumed that there would be plenty of time for such things on the voyage. I asked the captain whether the purser normally brought along his "lady friend." He said no. In reply to my question of how long the woman intended to remain with us he said that there were only two options, either she could disembark at Mold Bay or else go all the way to Izmit, because those would seemingly be our first two ports of call. But we would see how it went. I should mention that the purser was in his forties; a likable chap, despite an inability to pronounce his "r"s, who could be described as good-looking were it not for the milky-white cataract in his right eye. His foreign mistress was about twenty years younger than him.

There were seven of us in the saloon and plenty of room at the captain's table. Everyone was friendly and did their best to make this first meal as congenial as possible. I myself was not feeling quite the thing after my afternoon nap; there seemed to be something wrong with the heating in my cabin, because however far I turned on the radiator it remained obstinately cold, whether I turned the tap at the top or the bottom. After the cheery fat cook had announced the evening's well-thought-out menu, I informed the captain of my problem. And also that when, having started up from my sleep around three, I went into the saloon and complained to the ship's steward who was there polishing the dinner service, he had said that there were often small teething troubles with new ships, though of course this shouldn't happen, and that this little hitch would be sorted out in no time. However, this had not been done and now, you see, I was rather dreading the onset of night. Captain Alfredson nodded during my speech but did not reply, keeping his own counsel, but then signaled to the engineer to see to the matter. The engineer asked the company to excuse him and rose from the table.

Now the meal commenced with one splendid dish succeeding another. They had not lied about the quality of the Kronos line's cooking. What did attract my attention, however, was the fact that none of the dishes were fish. I thought to myself that this was probably coincidence and that we would have fish for the next four days as was customary in the Jung-Olsen family home. Anyway, it was all delightful and time passed far too quickly. The first engineer reappeared as we were finishing the most ambrosial *ris à la mande* that has ever passed my lips. He said he thought there was some grit in the radiator pipes, they must have come like that from the manufacturer, and he had ordered the third engineer to flush them out—or scrape them. I didn't entirely follow the details of this repair story—to tell the truth I considered it rather inappropriate for the dinner table. At this point Spanish brandy was served, accompanied by Danish cigars in a hardwood box, and without another word on the subject, the first engineer applied himself to these refreshments. Different rules pertain at sea from on shore—here men must constantly tend to their lodging even while enjoying its protection.

•

Sailors who have been at sea for many years have a bottomless supply of tales about events they have either experienced firsthand or heard of from others of their ilk. In particular, it turned out that Caeneus, second mate of the MS *Elizabet Jung-Olsen*, was not shy about sharing with us various incidents that had befallen him in his day. He did so for the entertainment of his messmates, though they regarded it as an education too, since he had traveled farther and seen more than any of them. From the anticipation that gripped my traveling companions I gathered that the second mate must be an outstanding storyteller, and I realized that they had been waiting for this moment throughout the meal.

I haven't touched tobacco since my wife died, as I explained to the captain so he wouldn't take it amiss when I declined his expensive cigars. However, I did accept another glass of brandy, then leaned back in my chair and prepared to enjoy Caeneus's seafaring yarn.

Before embarking on his tales the mate had the habit of drawing a rotten chip of wood from his pocket and holding it to his right ear like a telephone receiver. He would listen to the chip for a minute or two, closing his eyes as if asleep, while under his eyelids his pupils quivered to and fro. As this was the first time I had heard Caeneus talk, I smiled foolishly at his absurd performance. I could only assume that it was the prelude to some vulgar piece of clowning and mimicry, and I looked around, expecting to see the same reaction from my table companions—even to see the woman tittering. But they were sitting quite still in their seats, waiting for the story to begin. Even the purser's lady friend watched enthralled as the man listened to the splinter of wood. My smile swiftly faded and in my confusion I darted a glance at Captain Alfredson, who did me the courtesy of overlooking my faux pas. Abruptly leaning forward on his elbows, he said in a quiet, firm voice:

"It's where he gets the story from . . ."

At these words the second mate put down the piece of driftwood. And began his tale:

"Many things can befall a sailor in his life; the perils await him not only at sea but also in far-off ports. I wish to tell you about a train of events that led me into a piece of foolishness, which resulted in such misfortune that I came within an inch of losing my life.

"I was a deckhand on a ship called the *Argo*. We were crossing the Aegean, having set sail from the city of Iolcus in Magnesia with a long voyage ahead. The ship was newly built and fitted out with the finest rigging, but contrary winds and an unusually heavy swell had caused us to drift somewhat off our course at the very outset of our adventure. When we made landfall on the island of Lemnos it was with the intention of taking on water and provisions—there was certainly no other plan—and it should by rights have detained us no more than a couple of days. But in the event we were to spend nearly ten months on the island.

"Admittedly, we thought it strange that there were no ships lying in the harbor and that we hadn't encountered any craft in the approaches to the port, but as we were eager to reach land it was not enough to rouse our suspicions and make us cautious. Nor were we troubled by the fact that the docks were empty of people. The men exchanged glances and said that the citizens must be in the city celebrating some festival—and wasn't it a happy coincidence that we should turn up at such a time? We put out a boat and two of the crew piloted the ship to the harbor side. There we reefed the mainsail, moored the ship, and stepped ashore.

"The first reaction of a man who has come ashore from the sea is to wonder that the earth should be so firm beneath his feet. This lasts for an instant before being succeeded by another sensation that feels as if it will never end: thirst. In an instant all the salt that one has inhaled from the sea air is released from one's lungs to crystallize on the tongue, coating it like a glittering iron glove. And only one thing can quench that fire: wine.

"We looked as one man at the captain, who was standing by the gangway with the helmsman, and our eyes flashed with the eagerness of athletes at the starting line. A whole lifetime passed in this way, ending when the captain folded his arms across his chest and slowly shook his head. We emitted a pained sigh, the happy hopefulness fell from our faces, our shoulders drooped. The helmsman looked from this wretched rabble to his captain, who gave a sly smile. The helmsman laughed aloud. And the captain shouted at us, his white teeth flashing in the burning midday sun:

" 'By holy Dionysus, men, go forth and be merry!'

"And we answered in chorus:

" 'Long live the son of Aeson, long live Captain Jason!'

"It should be mentioned here that this crew con-sisted of no weaklings, but of the greatest heroes known to man. Each and every one of us could have steered an entire fleet to victory, each and every one of us had the courage to meet whatever foes may be, whether of hu-man or monstrous kind, but before thirst, even the great-est champions must concede defeat. We raced off up the wharf, for all the world like a swarm that has found the rotting carcass of an ass in a cabbage bed, making a beeline for the first tavern that met our eyes, and charged over the threshold with a great yell of jubilation. But our joy was short-lived, the yell died on our lips: it was a ghost town, there was nothing here but a layer of dust covering the benches and tables. We broke into the next tavern, and the next and the next; everywhere the same sight met our eyes.

"The wine barrels had burst and the long-desired drink moldered black as blood among the broken staves.

"Oh, the disappointment!

"We turned on our heels and trudged back to the ship with aggrieved complaint. When Jason son of Aeson saw his sailors returning to the quay so woebegone he grew thoughtful. And on hearing that the dock area had suc-cumbed to moths and rust, he ordered us to prepare without delay for battle with the monster that had evi-dently destroyed all human life on the island. He sent Phalerus, skilled in feats of arms, into the city to spy it out and with him the huntress Atalanta, the only woman among our number. They were well armed, as always, when there was the prospect of a hunt.

"These two had not gone far before they returned to the ship leading between them a golden-haired maid child that a group of terrified women had sent out to meet them. In her lily-white hand the girl held a papyrus scroll. The troop of armor-clad heroes stood aside, opening a path for the small maiden to the gangway where Jason greeted her. She handed him the scroll, which the son of Aeson unrolled and read with interest.

"The rest of us waited; soon we would know whether plague or a monster was responsible for the sinister state of the land. Meanwhile the stout midshipman Heracles set the child on his knee and performed tricks for her amusement."

•

I couldn't sleep that night. I had nodded during the second mate's story and finally fallen asleep, and in my dozing state the tale seemed to become ever more far-fetched. When the steward nudged me awake I was sitting alone at the captain's table in the saloon. All signs of the excellent repast had vanished.

I entered my cabin to find it baking hot. The first engineer's so-called repairs had involved no more than running scalding water into the radiators, then tightening the taps. To make matters worse the wind picked up from the northwest, accompanied by rough seas, so the ship, which was empty, began to roll and pitch. Chairs and other loose fittings took to the air, the drawers shot out of the chest, cupboard doors banged ceaselessly, and I was frantically engaged in trying to keep them under control until the early hours. When I finally managed to lie down, pouring with sweat under the empty quilt cover like an inhabitant of the tropics, a bustle began in the saloon: the whistling steward was preparing breakfast. I didn't have the strength to get up and give him a piece of my mind.

So clattering crockery and clinking cutlery formed my lullaby on my first "night" as a guest on board the flagship of my benefactor, Mr. Magnus Jung-Olsen.

III

That morning the MS *Elizabet Jung-Olsen* had cruised into Fedafjord, one of those endless Norwegian fjords, and now lay moored in a small bay at the foot of a lofty mountain. The settlement was a disgrace; shabby workers' huts had been thrown up higgledy-piggledy on the rock, with the sawmill and a large warehouse below. The only building worthy of the name of human habitation in this godforsaken hole was a yellow two-story house that stood at the end of the jetty. Meanwhile the gold—colossal tree trunks in their hundreds—floated in the bay.

After lunch I took a turn about the deck. I had a headache from the vicissitudes of the night before and was feeling lethargic following a midday meal of horse sausage with mashed potatoes and white sauce, but I found relief in watching the production of the paper pulp that was to be our cargo on this trip. Two steel cables ran from the mill and warehouse up to the summit of the mountain, which towered a thousand feet above the seedy little settlement. I was informed that from there the cables ran overhead straight to the doors of a timber-working factory located ten miles away up the long, tapering valley. I watched the workmen dragging the tree trunks up the beach, loading them on sleds, and sliding them into the mill. There the monster logs were chopped into chips and the chips were put into wagons, which then rolled along the cable that carried them up the valley to the factory. After the wood chips had been shredded, pulped, blended with this and that chemical, and pressed into sheets, they returned as ironbound blocks of raw paper, running back down the cable that ended up in the warehouse by the wharf. There the raw paper was stacked and finally loaded on board the ships that came from every direction to transport it around the globe.

I anticipated spending many happy hours watching the fresh wood chips ascending the mountain and vanishing over the top, while the snow-white paper pulp materialized over the edge and swooped majestically down the slopes.

The freight rate was fifty kroner per ton, according to Captain Alfredson, and our intention was to take on 2,500 tons of raw paper and transport it to the Black Sea coast of Turkey. I found a good spot to sit and wrapped myself in blankets. It pleased me to be able to witness with my own eyes the fortunes of my friends the Jung-Olsen family swelling with every pallet that the crane swung on board that happy ship the MS *Elizabet Jung-Olsen*. In fact, the day before I embarked, a report on their prosperity had made headline news in the *Stock Exchange Times*:

> The board of the Kronos shipping company has reported a profit from its operations last year, 1948, of 4,794,388.00 kroner. To this should be added the interest of 1,162,168.00 kroner which, after the addition of last year's arrears of 738,806.00 kroner, makes a total income of 6,693,357.00 kroner. After the overheads of 1,258,022.00 kroner, including dockyard fees in Denmark and elsewhere for maintenance and repairs to the fleet, are paid off, there will be a surplus of 5,450,000.00 kroner, which the annual general meeting of the company has agreed to allocate as follows: profit to shareholders 20 percent, payment to the new buildings fund 3,000,000.00 and, to be carried over to next year's account, 985,355.00 kroner, while a sum has already been set aside in a special fund to cover payment of taxes and foreign currency fluctuations. The company currently has at its disposal 16 steam or diesel vessels and 4 ships under construction. Profit to shareholders in 1947 was 12.5 percent.

At coffee time the purser's lady friend brought me some refreshments on deck, a selection of rations in a wicker basket with a dishcloth folded over the contents.

I had a better impression of her now than I had the previous night, having grown more accustomed to those goggling eyes and finding it evident from her general deportment that she had been well brought up, no matter where she crossed paths with the purser at the end of the war. She asked me warily whether it was right that I had been in Germany during the hostilities. I admitted as much and told her the truth; that I had worked for the German national broadcasting service, reading the news in Icelandic. She told me in turn that she had been a governess, a *Gouvernante*, on a country estate in Poland when war broke out and had remained there to the bitter end.

We conducted our conversation in German, for it had been a misunderstanding on my part that she knew any Danish (or that the purser spoke any German, for that matter), and she told me how badly the Germans had behaved after their arrival in Poland.

"First they broke all the windows in the house by throwing stones, then after that, they started on the family furnishings, the furniture and dinner service, not stopping until everything had been smashed to smithereens.

"The filth and squalor were so appalling that it was too much to bear, even for a person trained in home economics like myself. Many of the soldiers had been wounded and the dressings on their wounds hadn't been touched for weeks. Their clothes were in a disgusting state, but instead of washing them, they just threw them on the fire when use and dirt had worn them away. Then the soldier who was immediately subordinate in rank would have the clothes torn off his back, if they fitted his superior and were not complete *Scheiße*—please excuse the phrase—and so on down the line until some poor Pole was shot for his rags.

"And their eating habits were no better. The Germans fed themselves with their bare hands, and if large chunks of meat were on offer they would throw themselves on them, ripping and tearing until the whole place was awash with brawling and a large part of the meal went to waste. Afterward it took them hours to lick the remnants of food from their hands, since they had rings on every finger (all looted from the living and the dead) and it required some skill to suck the scraps of meat, grease, and blood from under the rings, where it would rot if it wasn't eaten—those same hands that they laid on the womenfolk."

She omitted to mention how the Russians had behaved when they entered Poland some years later and the fact that she didn't touch on that side of the matter roused my suspicions that she was not entirely impartial. But I didn't comment on it at the time because she pointed a plump finger at the basket and said:

"Please, don't let it get cold . . ."

Once she was out of sight I whipped the dishcloth

27

off the basket to discover a thermos of milky tea, which was indeed going cold, and a diagonally cut ham sandwich on a glass plate.

So as yet there was no letup in the carnivorous eating habits on board the MS *Elizabet Jung-Olsen*.

•

Entrée
Thinly sliced roast beef
with pickled gherkins and cold potato salad

Main Course
Pork shanks in red wine
with red cabbage, Brussels sprouts, and wild
mushroom sauce

Dessert
Raspberry and rhubarb compote
with whipped cream

After the dinner guests had sung the cook's praises for this tasty but indigestible meal it was time for the evening's entertainment. This was a continuation of yesterday's story, which was apparently not yet finished. The second mate took out the piece of wood, performed the same spectacle as the night before, and in the dead silence that settled on the saloon resumed his tale:

"The message the young maiden brought Jason, our

captain, was from Queen Hypsipyle, the doe-eyed beauty who ruled over Lemnos. According to this letter, the men of the island had moved away to Thrace, judging the women of that land both fairer and more submissive than their own wives. They had sailed from the island under cover of night, taking with them all their sons and killing any male slaves. The only male creature they left behind alive was Hypsipyle's aged father, King Thoas. And he had not been alone with the daughters of Lemnos for long before he, too, fled on the only vessel he could push from land unaided; a chest containing the undergarments of Hypsipyle's handmaidens. Yes, things had come to such a pass that when we landed on Lemnos it was inhabited solely by women.

"It is a widespread belief that sailors have a girl-friend in every port but that's an exaggeration. Far from having a girlfriend in *every* port we usually have them in only one or two—well, maybe three or four. Naturally, there are disadvantages to this arrangement, though the will is ever present; it depends on the countries and the native customs as to how willing their womenfolk are to accommodate strangers. For although it is pretty much the rule that sailors go ashore to find themselves a woman, this aim can miscarry in some ports. And worst of all are the times when part of the crew must set sail again without having experienced an hour of bliss in the arms of some compliant beauty, since this can lead to bad feeling between those who got lucky and those who did not. Such discord among the crew is something that no captain would wish for.

"A manly smile played over the lips of Jason son of Aeson. Looking boldly to shore, he raised the papyrus scroll to the skies and shouted in triumph:

"'My friends, we find ourselves on an island of women!'

"The news left us speechless.

"Before being overwhelmed by the contrary winds that brought us to Lemnos, our ship, the *Argo*, had cleft the seas like a gull that skims the surface, the crests of the waves wetting the tips of its wings while the bird itself glides between sky and sea like wing-footed Hermes, the messenger of the gods. And all the while that miraculous musician Orpheus strummed the rhythm on his lyre, chanting a lay that caused the monsters of the deep to flinch away from the eager prow of our many-nailed craft in the very act of attacking. For the *Argo* appeared to these monsters like some divine being, a unique life force, the song and the singer, a new verb that combined the verbs 'to come' and 'to go,' at once both mother and womb—for the embryo always believes that the mother is nothing more than her womb. And we oarsmen were truly the *Argo*'s children. We braced against the blocks and rowed in contest with the hostile wind that filled the mainsail, twenty-four to a side, two to a bench, applying ourselves to the oars, dragging them back and swinging them forward—back and forth, as if grappling with an energetic bedmate. The ship flew over the water, rocking her crew, and the way she rose and fell on her way across the choppy highways of the barren sea strongly recalled the rolling hips of Aphrodite as she took to the waves in her scallop shell.

"Such was the loverlike tempo that had taken up residence in the virile bodies of the Argonauts during their voyage; such was the rhythm that governed our movements when we found dry land under our feet at last.

"And the women of Lemnos had been alone a long time . . ."

Here the second mate paused in his narrative and reached for the water jug. His audience sighed gustily and sipped their drinks, pleased with the story so far. Meanwhile, I seized this opportunity to put a question to the evening's guest of honor, Raguel Bastesen, the director of the paper mills (he claimed Icelandic descent through a grandmother from Hnífsdalur), saying by way of a preamble:

"Today I have been looking down the fjord, or perhaps up it, I simply can't work out which is which. I can't for the life of me understand where the entrance is to this bowl we're sitting in. When I asked Captain Alfredson this morning which direction we had entered the fjord from—by your leave, Captain—he answered by pointing due north, to where the rock wall is at its highest. But I couldn't see any gap by which we could have entered, nor can the MS *Elizabet Jung-Olsen*—excellent ship as she is—sail straight through the Norwegian *fjeld*."

My dinner companions gave a murmur of laughter at this last sally. I tilted my head, looking waggishly at Captain Alfredson to ensure that everyone knew the joke was on me, not him. And added:

"You see, I assumed we had come from the south, where the mountains are lowest."

Then I came to my question:

"So I appeal to you, Herr Director, as a local; what species of fish are most common in this fjord?"

To my astonishment Raguel Bastesen seemed at a loss:

"Er, that's a good question . . ." the director muttered, plucking at his right earlobe and rubbing it between finger and thumb while he considered his answer. I filled the gap:

"You see, it occurred to me that we might be able to purchase some fresh fish for the pot."

At this he seemed to wake up:

"Oh, no, I doubt that, Mr. Haraldsson, fish don't find their way up here in any great number. It's mainly in April that you get a shoal or two of cod straying into the fjord by mistake. Then you can catch the odd fish with a rod, some of them quite large, but we don't see any other species."

I had difficulty hiding my disappointment at Director Bastesen's "neither nor" reply. My dinner companions were not especially concerned, having shown nothing but satisfaction with the catering on board, so I thanked him politely and the captain gave the mate Caeneus a sign to resume his tale, which he did:

"Our ship was the *Argo* of the many nails, the greatest vessel of her age. The timbers of her hull came from the forests of Mount Pelion, where Jason son of Aeson had been fostered until the age of twenty by Master Cheiron, Cheiron's mother, his wife, and his daughters— and this Cheiron was half man, half horse, or what the poets call a 'centaur.' The trees of the forest containing the future strakes of the yet-to-be-built ship were felled under the guidance of this same Cheiron, who chose only those trees that had achieved their full maturity during the time the future captain of our ship had shared the mountain with them. Indeed, while their branches had been stretching their leafy crowns to the skies and their roots sucked nourishment from the fertile soil of the Pelion heights, the young Jason's muscles had been tempered by the practice of sports on the mountainsides by day, while by night his intellectual gifts were honed in debate and song in the deep cavern of his tutor.

"Yet although Jason's mind and hand had such a deep rapport with the vessel that he was to steer, it was evident that it would require more than mere mortal strength to achieve the superhuman task that had been laid upon us. So the day the ship was deemed ready to launch, bright-eyed Athena descended to Earth among the shipwrights and fitted in her prow a beam from the whispering oak of her father, Zeus. With this gift the *Argo* became the eighth wonder of the world, and the speaking bow timber was to be our guide throughout the perilous quest that lay ahead.

"Now the bow timber had some motherly advice for Jason son of Aeson, captain of the *Argo*, telling him to order his crew back on board and continue on his way. Gently but firmly she reminded him that by our hazardous voyage into the blue grasp of Poseidon the Earthshaker, who could easily twiddle the greatest galley in the world like a penny between his blue fingers—by this voyage, we Argonauts were intending to be the first men ever to negotiate the Clashing Rocks. For thus we would enter the Black Sea to reach the land of Colchis and find the Golden Fleece that Jason's people had lost and wished to recover. They had promised to make him king if he fulfilled this quest.

"But as Jason son of Aeson stood foursquare on the gangway with the message from doe-eyed Hypsipyle in his upraised hand, he was deaf to the ship's voice of reason. The queen of Lemnos had concluded her letter with the words that he was welcome to a banquet at her palace together with those of his crew who were not standing watch that evening. So now Jason ordered us Argonauts to ready ourselves for a visit to the nation of women.

"Jason buckled on his purple mantle of double fold, a gift he had received from the hand of Athena the day the keel was laid in our ship, the *Argo*, and this mantle was a creation of such blazing splendor that it rivaled the dawn; red as fire in the middle, deepening to indigo at the richly illustrated hem. This hem was embroidered with gold and told the story of the siblings Phrixus and Helle, children of King Athamas and the cloud goddess Nephele. When their stepmother, Ino, convinced their father that he should sacrifice his children to prevent the harvest from failing in the land of Iolcus, they escaped on the back of a certain golden-fleeced talking ram.

"Having flown a longish way, the children began to tire and it so chanced that midway the girl Helle fell to Earth over the Sea of Marmara, which has been known ever since as the Hellespont. But at the ram's urging the boy Phrixus clung on for dear life to his dazzling woolly coat and so at last they reached land at Colchis. There the boy married the princess, sacrificed the ram, and dedicated the sacrifice to the war god, Ares. He hung the blazing gold fleece in a grove of trees, casting a web of spells so that it would be guarded by a sleepless dragon and no man would ever be able to lay hands on it. Meanwhile, back in Iolcus, the children's homeland, the people thought it a national disgrace to have lost the fabled ram into the clutches of the men of Colchis.

"All these events could be seen woven into our captain Jason's purple cloak. And where the story of Phrixus and Helle ended, his own story began.

"Jason son of Aeson now set out to meet doe-eyed

Hypsipyle, the powerful queen of the Lemnian women, together with the poet Orpheus, the beekeeper Butes, and the brothers Zetes and Calais, the winged sons of Boreas. The mantle swirled about the captain's body—how well he wore it!—while the dazzling storied web billowed about his feet as if he were floating like an immortal on a sun-flushed cloud. Toward evening the rest of us were to march through the town and meet them in the palace gardens.

"So, with the help of the finery that we had brought along in our kit bags, we deckhands hurriedly set about making ourselves presentable for the womenfolk of Lemnos."

IV

Today there was an accident at the sawmill. I was sitting in my spot on deck with one eye on the cable cars that were crawling up and down the mountain as they had the day before, the other on the fishing rod that I had cadged from the purser. I had baited the hook with bully beef, cast the line over the port side, and fixed the rod firmly to the gunwale. The line glittered as it arced gently in the spring breeze. My gaze was fixed on the float when the factory siren suddenly set up a deep strident wailing in the bay—and a moment later there was a clank from the mountainside: the cableway had ground to a halt, timber wagons swaying on one side, ironbound blocks of paper on the other.

A workman in blue overalls came racing out of the mill and ran over to the yellow two-story house where the director, Raguel, had his headquarters. Two clerks came out to meet him. The workman waved his arms in the air, pointing to the sawmill and the yellow house in turn. Then he clenched his fist and held it to his ear as if talking on the phone, at which one of the clerks ran back into the house, while the worker and the other clerk raced back to the mill. As they reached it the big doors at the eastern end were flung open and four factory hands hurried out carrying a fifth on a stretcher between them. He seemed delirious and kept trying to throw himself off the stretcher while his workmates pushed him down again. He beat them off with what seemed like unusually short arms that I understood later had been truncated in the accident—torn off at the elbows. More workmen came out of the mill doors on their heels and looked on apprehensively. One turned, shouted something to the others, and pointed to the cable cars.

Now the door of one of the workers' huts burst open and a wailing woman tried to run to the injured man but before she could go far the man in blue overalls intercepted her and clasped her tight. Three young children appeared in the doorway and stood there watching their mother cry, not daring to venture out.

I heard a truck start up on the quay and a moment later it drove over to the group by the mill. The driver shouted something out the window to the stretcher-bearers but they didn't stir. At that, the office clerk from the yellow house did some fast talking, gesticulating with his arms and stamping his feet, trying to drag the others over to the back of the truck. The man holding the woman now relinquished his task to someone else, shouted an order at the stretcher-bearers, and ran to the beetle-black limousine parked beside the yellow house; it was the director's own car, a Chrysler Windsor, 1947 vintage.

I nudged the first engineer, who was standing beside me on deck watching the events unfold like the rest of the crew of the MS *Elizabet Jung-Olsen*.

"This should be interesting . . ."

The man in blue overalls tore open the rear door of the director's car and the others hurried over with the amputee. Meanwhile, the office clerk cupped his hands around his mouth and flung back his head, bellowing for all he was worth at the upstairs windows of the yellow house. As the men began to ease their bleeding workmate into the limousine its owner appeared at one of the office windows. He yelled and brandished his fist at the workmen, but pretending not to notice, they continued with their rescue effort. Next moment Herr Bastesen was down in the garage, ready to defend his pride and joy, moving extraordinarily nimbly, I thought, for such a fat man. He was about to grab one of the four workers by the shoulder when the man in blue overalls intervened and drove his clenched fist under the director's nose with such careless force that the fellow crumpled to the ground unconscious.

At that the entire crew of the MS *Elizabet Jung-Olsen* (including the purser's lady friend) broke into applause—for I was not the only one who didn't care for Raguel Bastesen. Captain Alfredson, unable to join in with his men by virtue of his position, contented himself with coughing "ahem" several times into his chest. I meanwhile said as if to myself but loud enough for others to hear:

"Good, good . . ."

Throughout this sorry spectacle the factory siren had been wailing unremittingly and did not let up until the car vanished from view in a cloud of dust over the shoulder of the mountain. Then everything became so quiet that in the ensuing silence the hearts of the onlookers on deck were filled with sadness and shame at their failure to act, though one couldn't really have done anything to help. Captain Alfredson cleared his throat and uttered a single word:

"Men!"

It was enough to make the crew return wordlessly to their former tasks. That left just the two of us, the mate Caeneus, who was off duty, and I, who was a supernumerary, to watch the aftermath. Bastesen's clerks lugged their supine boss up the steps of the yellow house. The young children stood in the hut doorway, supporting one another, until the man who was looking after their mother led her inside, closing the door behind them.

I moved closer to Mate Caeneus, took up position at his side, and gripped the rail like him. He nodded to me but somehow I sensed he was looking at my hands. I nodded back and returned the favor. It was only then that I realized just what a big fellow the mate was. At the dinner table I had thought we were of a similar build, in spite of the age difference, but now it became clear that he was your average man multiplied by 1.23 ($5'6'' \times 1.23 = 6'9''$ tall), and his bulk was consistent with this. I have always been considered a strapping fellow but Caeneus was a titan. And it was all muscle that rippled beneath his mate's jacket.

Having finished my examination, I said in a casually conversational tone:

"Well."

"Yes," he responded.

"So it goes."

"Yes."

"Life in Norway . . ."

"I s'pose so . . ." he said.

I changed the subject:

"That's quite a story you tell the crew in the evenings."

"You said it . . ."

"They seem to enjoy it, for all its oddness."

There was a short pause—a black-headed gull flew overhead.

"Anyway . . ."

With that the broad-shouldered Caeneus raised his index finger to touch his scalp on the right in a brief salute and took his leave:

"Thanks for the chat, Mr. Haraldsson."

I hesitated a moment. As the mate tilted his head, his

eyes twinkled like a woman's. Having seen some pretty odd things in Berlin in the years after the First World War, I thought:

"Aha . . ."

But said merely:

"Thank *you*!"

And raised my left hand halfway to my temple. Caeneus headed to the bridge while I returned aft to tend to my rod.

I was in luck: a huge cod had taken the bait and swum far out into the bay with the line. There it was fighting to free itself from the hook, bending the rod to breaking point for what seemed like an eternity—it took me a full forty minutes to reel it in. When it finally stopped flapping about the deck and lay gasping at my feet, I calculated that this gargantuan fish would suffice for at least two meals for the seven of us at the captain's table.

·

The diners raised their eyebrows when the main course was served that evening. It consisted of poached cod and potatoes with melted butter and slices of tomato. The cook emerged from the galley to inform the dinner guests that I'd come up with this recipe off the top of my head and had told him that on the rare occasions when Hermann Jung-Olsen and I had had the good fortune to dine together this was the dish that had been served, though sometimes with haddock instead of cod.

"Quite right!" I said, though I pointed out that the tomatoes were the cook's idea, and the only accompaniment apart from potatoes that the late Hermann and I had eaten with this dish was dulse. Most of the diners tucked in with gusto and a voice was heard to comment that this made an unexpected change from the ship's customary menu.

Whether it was thanks to this light but substantial fare or not, a novelty occurred in that Mate Caeneus took up his tale between the main course and dessert:

"That evening we trooped to Queen Hypsipyle's palace, where they were throwing a great banquet in honor of Jason and his Argonauts. The streets were lined with the skirt-clad populace of Lemnos: civilian women, crook-backed bondswomen, and giggling young girls, all hungrily eyeing the troop of heroes who passed through the city like molten lead in the crucible of Hephaestus, glowing hotly in their molded, sun-burnished armor, eager to harden in the tempering embrace of the court ladies. The only thing that detracted from the magnificence of the occasion was the powerful stench that filled the streets like steam from a bathhouse, the iron smell of blood mingling with the sweetness of cow dung, the sour reek of burnt wood in the rain and the bitterness of apricot kernels.

"We breathed through our mouths, hoping the miasma

would disperse when we emerged from the close-packed houses. But when we drew near the palace and the stench proved even more pungent there and worst of all in the banqueting hall, where the women awaited us, we realized that it originated in none other than the reed-soft bodies of the ladies we had come to meet. From innate courtesy both men and women pretended not to notice the stink. Doe-eyed Hypsipyle ordered her court ladies to form a line and Jason ordered his crew to do the same. Once this was done one of the maidens stepped forward and curtseyed and the crew member standing opposite her stepped up to join her and bowed, then she took his hand and led him to a seat in the hall, and so on down the line until there was no one left but Jason and Hypsipyle, who bowed simultaneously, he lower still, and then walked hand in hand to the throne.

"Great was the relief of both sexes when the stench evaporated the instant the hands of man and woman met. For with our arrival and willingness to touch such noxious-smelling women we had unwittingly broken the spell on our gentle hostesses. They told us that as a punishment for driving away their husbands, Aphrodite had put a spell on the women of Lemnos so they would give off such a putrid stench that no man would wish to come within three hundred paces of them. The reason for the spiteful nature of this curse was that Aphrodite's husband, that clumsy cuckold Hephaestus, held sway on Lemnos and the women had always diligently tended his temple with sacrificial gifts and paeans. But Aphrodite envied her husband the attention and had long sought a means to harm the women. Yet now it transpired that in devising her vengeful gift the busy goddess of love and underhand dealings had forgotten that a long sea voyage renders all women equal in a sailor's eyes . . ."

Here Caeneus broke off, raising his eyebrows to the roots of his hair and waiting for his shipmates' reaction.

"Yes, don't we know it!" piped up the first engineer.

And the crew of the MS *Elizabet Jung-Olsen* bubbled over with laughter. Whereas I, the purser's lady friend, and the purser himself (after being elbowed by his lady friend) lowered our eyes and waited for the mate to resume his tale, which he did after the men had got over their mirth:

"At the banqueting tables, on the Argonauts' first evening on the Island of Women, we were entertained with an epic from the lands north of the river Istrus. The poet was a slender, long-limbed woman who plucked a pearl-inlaid lyre in accompaniment to her song. Her corn-yellow hair was cut short, locks the length of a handspan rippling about her head like waves on a shore. About her shoulders she wore a black shawl that covered her arms down to the backs of her hands, where it was fastened to her middle fingers with silver rings. There were no pictures on this costume, but the poetess drew her song from its dark weave and the themes were all as somber in color as the night; the jests evoked a raven's wing dipped in pitch, while the reality that underpinned them was bottomless, as the pupil in a hate-filled eye.

"Her poem told of the hapless hero Sigurd who slighted his wife, the sorceress Gudrun, by planning to take a new wife, the princess Brynhild. He told Gudrun that this would be in the best interests of their sons, Gjuki and Hogni. Sigurd made a pact with Brynhild's father, King Grim, that Gudrun should be allowed to go into exile with a generous purse while their sons remained with him and Brynhild took their mother's place. Naturally, his actions were motivated by consideration for the boys and had nothing to do with the young princess's downy soft bosom or virginal rose-pink flesh. This arrangement was all the greater betrayal of Gudrun since she had cast off everything that is dearest—her father, homeland, and younger brother—in order to follow Sigurd wherever the goddesses of fate led them.

"The black-clad poetess began her song by describing how Sigurd and Gudrun fell in love when he raided the coast of her homeland, intending to carry off a swan's-feather cloak of white silver that hung in the sacred grove of Freyja, guarded by the poisonous serpent Fafnir. There was no getting past this monster except by witchcraft—and no one knew this black art better than Gudrun, who at the time was both daughter to the king of the land and also a priestess of Hel.

"In Sigurd's retinue were three goddesses who traveled with him unseen. These were Frigg, Sif, and Freyja, who vied among themselves as to who had the most power over the mortal man's fate. Freyja caused one of her cats to scratch Gudrun, who was so consumed by the fires of love that she became unhealthily enamored of Sigurd. That night the two of them stole to Freyja's temple and the king's daughter lulled the dragon to sleep while Sigurd drew his halberd and struck the monster a blow under the pinion as she had taught him. At that the hideous Fafnir started up and blasted out a terrible poison, but thanks to Gudrun's intervention it did the hero no harm. From this deed Sigurd won the title of 'Fafnir's bane.' He now snatched up the feather cloak of glittering silver, which had the property of endowing whoever wore it with the gift of flight like a bird.

"Gudrun was forced to flee with her lover, taking her brother Helgi with her, while King Gjuki gave chase with thirteen swift-sailing ships. To delay his pursuit, Gudrun killed Helgi, dismembered his body, and threw it into the sea, so that their father, Gjuki, would have to pause in his voyage to gather up the remains of his son. In this manner the lovers, Sigurd Fafnir's-bane and Gudrun Gjukadóttir, made their escape.

"At this point in the epic the daughters of Lemnos laughed cynically, and the poetess rested her long fingers on the strings of her lyre until their laughter had died away. Meanwhile, we men seized our cups and raised them to our lips to drown the nausea that rose in our throats.

"How could their womanly hearts take pleasure in such a sickening tale?

"By the time the nectar had soothed my throat the women's laughter had ceased and I glanced at the maiden beside me. She was waiting, expressionless and still, for my response, and when I managed to force my lips into a curve she smiled sweetly back, stroking my hip—before her eyes, wet with tears of mirth, flickered from mine to resettle obediently on the poetess, who now resumed her strumming. The second half of the story was even uglier than the first.

"It told of Sigurd's homecoming.

"After voyaging over strange and perilous seas he returned to his fatherland to exchange the silver-plumed treasure for the kingdom in accordance with the bargain he had struck with King Attila before he left. But Attila laughed at Sigurd and broke the pact, saying: 'Take your stinking swanskin and spread it under Gudrun Gjukadóttir next time you lie with her. Then you will know the color of her blood—for black on white is easily seen!'

"Thus King Attila insulted Sigurd Fafnir's-bane, sitting tightly ensconced on the throne that the hero had intended for himself and his wife. And Sigurd had to endure the humiliation of being denied the kingdom in spite of having retrieved the priceless swanskin. The men who had sailed with him to the end of the world now turned their backs on him; the crowd who had welcomed Sigurd as their new king on his homecoming now whispered ever louder about the devilish arts employed by his foreign bride-to-be for the theft: indeed, what they had once called recovery they now termed plunder—and Sigurd's men had no wish to be associated with a thief.

"But Gudrun Gjukadóttir did not stop there in her eagerness to help Sigurd Fafnir's-bane. She became a regular guest at the palace, where she enchanted Attila's daughters, Gunnhild and Hildigunn, with her flattery and magic. In their youth and naïveté they were taken in by the foreign woman's honeyed words—for she was both exotic and sinister in a way that titillates the young—and as is common with teenagers, the princesses despised their father as old and behind the times. He was ancient, nearly fifty! They were ashamed of him, and so were delighted when the beautiful enchantress said she knew a way to make King Attila young and virile again.

"On the appointed day, Gudrun Gjukadóttir went to the palace, armed with an ax and a large cauldron. She sat herself down in the middle of the banqueting hall, filled the cauldron with herbs and water, and lit a good fire underneath. Then she led a black billy goat into the hall and chopped it up into seven pieces with the ax, hacking head and limbs from the trunk, which she then cut in two and placed in the pot. As the cauldron boiled, bubbled, and flashed red in the steam, the witch chanted her ancient incantations, stirring the soup all the while. After a brief space she thrust an arm into the cauldron and drew out a bleating kid. It was black, with the same white star on its forehead as the old billy goat, which seemed to have been reborn before the eyes of those present. The princesses clapped their hands and twirled around: the time had come for their aged father to be rejuvenated by the same charm.

"The daughters of Lemnos gloated over his fate but it pierced our Argonaut hearts to hear such gruesome events treated as entertainment. However, mindful of the women's unspoken, and far from guaranteed, promises of unconditional compliance, we took care not to offend them with our dismay.

"The poetess was darker than our Lemnian hostesses. Her skin took on a blue sheen as she plucked the pearl-inlaid lyre, her body swaying back and forth with the rhythm, the shawl at times veiling the fair-voiced poetess and her instrument like a coal-green wave. And so the third part of the story began. The woman's deep voice resonated from within the gossamer twilight of her veil as she performed for us the denouement of the tale:

"Sigurd Fafnir's-bane and Gudrun Gjukadóttir were living in exile after the murder of Attila. Gudrun was content, having borne him two promising sons, Hogni and Gjuki, but Sigurd resented their poverty. He met Princess Brynhild while out walking one day and fell in love with her. She in turn was greatly impressed that such a widely renowned dragon slayer should want her for his wife. Together they convinced her father, Grim, that Sigurd had taken no part in Gudrun's appalling crimes and that he was a fitting guest for the royal palace and a worthy husband for Brynhild. As the poetess described the moment when Sigurd informed Gudrun of his intention to divorce her and send her away, as he was going to marry Brynhild and keep their sons, we men assumed that a lively marriage farce would now ensue in place of the gory tale of horror, so we laughed even louder than the women.

"What none of us knew that evening on Lemnos was that the song in which the dark poetess's voice was raised prophesied the fate of our beloved captain Jason—the hero who lost everything was none other than he.

"The day before Sigurd and Brynhild's wedding, Gudrun gave her sons by Sigurd a gift for their father's new bride; a deadly poisonous robe that would slay first Brynhild and then King Grim when he tried to save his daughter. It must have been the saddest hour of my life when I saw the flash of laughter in Jason's eyes, yes, he laughed out loud with Queen Hypsipyle when the song reached its climax in the description of how the scorned wife murdered her own children. For this deed Gudrun employed no sorcery, merely locked herself in the house with Hogni and Gjuki, Sigurd's sons, and hunted the little boys down before hacking them both to death with their father's halberd. After this Gudrun wrapped herself in the swan's-feather cloak and took to the skies, gleaming silver-white against the newly kindled winter moon. Sigurd Fafnir's-bane, meanwhile, gave way to despair and ended his days a beggar.

"Overcome with giggles, the sisters of Lemnos chimed in with the dusky poetess as she sang the final lines:

> Unquenchable and terrible is the hate
> that quickens when the fires of love abate.

"Of course, Jason was intoxicated with wine and the presence of the queen who lay pressed to his side, entwining him in her white arms and raising her left knee to lay it against his inner thigh—but in my heart I hope that he heard an echo of his future in the poem and hid his dread with this pretense so that the rest of us would not be daunted. Yet if it occurred to any of the sailors that the events of the poem had a strange resonance with the destination of the *Argo* and her valiant captain, the thought had evaporated like yesterday's rain shower by the time the men rose, befuddled and satisfied, from their couches. It was not until years later when we finally learned the truth about the terrible fate of the men of Lemnos that we understood why their womenfolk's humor was so black.

"That same night while the crew of the *Argo* lay with Hypsipyle's court ladies, the men who were guarding the ship witnessed a strange event. The lad Hylas, page of Heracles, told how at midnight a tall, dark, slender-limbed woman appeared on the shore. She walked with light steps to a bank of seaweed, drew from beneath it a silver-gray sealskin, swept it around herself, and made for the sea. A wave greeted her, enveloping the supple body like a green-black shawl, and the seal slipped away through the sea like a note leaping from the string of a lyre.

"This was the seal woman Psamathe, sister to the sea nymph Thetis, the same who piloted the *Argo* on her homeward voyage through the Straits of Messina where the she-monsters Scylla and Charybdis lay in wait beneath the cliffs on either side, eager to feast on our flesh."

V

On April 13 I noted in my diary that the weather was fine though a little nippy. I imagine there's a calm here most of the year round since we are enclosed by mountains, and I have difficulty working out where the wind could come from. It's as if we were in a funnel where only the upper airs are visible—and tangible, for here it can really bucket down with rain, as I discovered at noon when I came up on deck intending to fish for more cod.

Even if it hadn't been raining, any further attempt at fishing would have been hampered by my inability to find my tackle, though I had conscientiously put it away in a box full of marlinspikes and other such paraphernalia that stood in the corner behind the big capstan. I suspect the purser's lady friend of having a hand in this, as ever since our bang-up dinner yesterday evening she has been distinctly crabby, even actively hostile toward me. This morning when I came to the breakfast table she got up at once, asked the company to excuse her, and walked out of the saloon without a glance in my direction.

Her change of heart occurred after she saw me give the ship's cook (or "chef," as he's called) the big cod, which he then prepared and served according to my instructions. Today at lunchtime a soup was made from the head and bones, the chopped-up cheeks floating in stock with carrots, bay leaves, peppercorns, and onion, and yet there was still more than enough left over to make a fish stew for tonight's supper.

Anyway, the purser's lady friend seemed to regard this contribution of mine to our little community on board the MS *Elizabet Jung-Olsen* as a criticism of her boyfriend's job. And of course she was right that my actions were motivated by more than a mere appetite for seafood: I felt that on the maiden voyage of this new vessel of the Kronos line it would have done the purser credit to have been guided by Jung-Olsen and his son's ideals when it came to buying provisions—and he himself certainly took the hint and swallowed it without rancor. If anything, I would have expected his lady friend to be grateful to me for eking out their stores, thus enabling them to profit still further from the illicit trade in which they and the cook were engaged.

Last night I started awake at the sound of voices in the saloon. Although they were trying to be quiet, I overheard a business transaction that would not have tolerated the light of day: strange voices were haggling over the price of tinned ham but the purser's lady friend wasn't budging an inch. Apparently the problem is rife among the prosperous Danish shipping lines whose pursers and cooks make a killing by selling off provisions on the side; many of them even have regular customers in foreign ports. I don't know what the woman would do if she knew I had overheard the couple's secret commerce.

As luck would have it, three Norwegian police officers turned up here at coffee time to take statements from those of us who were on deck when the accident occurred at the factory. I voluntarily engaged the eldest in conversation, going so far as to appoint myself his escort while the visit lasted, thereby using an old ploy to alert the law to my presence on board the MS *Elizabet Jung-Olsen*. He was a man of about fifty, powerfully built and keen-eyed, with prematurely white hair, small ears, and the familiar-sounding moniker of Knud Hamsun:

"With a 'd' . . ." he said, explaining that he was no relation to the great writer.

I invited him to inspect my quarters and take my statement there, adding that I would like to offer him some Irish whiskey from a flask that the owner of Café Sommerfugl had given me as a parting gift when I set out on this voyage. As we went below I noticed that the officer had a limp and observed to him that it didn't really matter once you were on board ship; it merely looked as if he were riding the swell and no one would notice that he was different from the rest of us.

The taking of my statement was performed with a

civility that did the Norwegian officer credit. I gave Knud Hamsun a thorough description of all I had seen and heard, stressing, as was true, that Raguel Bastesen's reaction had been far from admirable; the injured man owed his life to his workmate, who had been forced to knock the director unconscious before he could use the car that would carry them most speedily to the hospital.

"Yes, I'm not afraid to say it, though I'm no friend of the Communists and have played a personal part in the struggle against them!"

The officer finished noting down my statement in shorthand in his leather-bound pocket book, which he then closed, snapping on a red elastic band and pushing the pencil stub underneath:

"I'm sorry to have to inform you that the worker Vidar Røyrvik died from his injuries this morning at the Kristiansand District Hospital."

"Oh . . ."

"Yes . . ."

Finishing his whiskey, Knud Hamsun continued:

"There's always a danger of unrest among the ranks of the dead man's fellow workers following incidents like this, so we've arrested the men who drove him to the hospital and announced that they are being held in custody until the investigation into the theft of the car is complete. There is nothing to prevent the factory from returning to work now, so there should be no further delay to your business here in Mold Bay."

On this positive note he concluded the taking of my statement, and we returned to the saloon, where the purser's lady friend, ignoring me, offered Officer Hamsun coffee and pancakes. I nudged him and made sure she was in earshot when I said:

"Hark, hark, the hen crows louder than the cock . . ."

By this means I made sure that he would be aware of the bad blood between the woman and me. Should anything happen to me before we continued on our voyage he was bound to recall this little incident. And my odd choice of words might even arouse his suspicions that the woman's generosity was designed to cover up some criminal activity. This didn't escape her, cunning creature that she was, and I felt we were now even.

I struck my brow lightly:

"Oh, I forgot! Would you excuse me? There's something I have to finish before evening . . ."

I parted from Knud Hamsun with a handshake and returned to my cabin. Now he would have a chance to get properly acquainted with the woman, untroubled by my presence. Or would he? Perhaps it hadn't been so clever to leave him with her after all? I realized all of a sudden how much the purser's lady friend resembled the temptresses of Lemnos described to us by Mate Caeneus in his evening yarns. And it dawned on me that her erratic behavior might indicate a breach in her relationship with the purser. Far from protecting him, as I had originally thought, she was on the hunt for a new man; someone who had more going for him than her unfortunate boyfriend—a man who could be her meal ticket to a better life.

So the bad feeling wasn't connected to the cod at all but had in fact begun when she brought me the snack with my coffee the day before yesterday. She had been very friendly at the time and opened her heart to me. Perhaps she was under the impression, since I'm staying in a two-room cabin suite that's almost the twin of Captain Alfredson's, that I must be a wealthy man. Could the purpose of her sob story have been to kindle pity in my aged breast? And afterward might she have intended to press her advantage and win both my love and my money? As soon as she made inquiries into my situation she would of course have discovered that I am only a poor Icelandic pensioner, a widower who has enough trouble supporting himself and lives alone in a poky rented apartment in Copenhagen, and not in the best part of town either. At that point she must have felt she had put herself at a disadvantage by making a play for me, resulting in a feeling of resentment, even animosity, toward me.

As I shut my cabin door I saw the purser's lady friend showing my ally Knud Hamsun to a seat at a table laid for coffee on the other side of the saloon. I only hoped his long experience in the police force would enable him to withstand her womanly wiles.

•

This evening it was at long last Mate Caeneus's turn to take the watch, and Captain Alfredson and I had agreed that after supper I would hold a lecture for the crew on fish and culture. The reason for this was twofold:

a) It was thanks to my publication of a journal on this subject that I was present on board as a special guest of the crew's ultimate superior, the shipping magnate Magnus Jung-Olsen.

b) It was thanks to my efforts at fishing that we were enjoying nutritious cod for our third meal in a row.

I declined the starter—egg mayonnaise with grated vegetables on a lettuce leaf—taking the opportunity to go over the opening of my speech instead. Although I can, without recourse to notes, deliver lengthy impromptu lectures on the relationship between fish consumption and culture, this evening's effort had to be rather better than that. After all, this was not my usual audience—the regulars at Café Sommerfugl—no, this time my lecture was to be delivered on board the flagship of the Kronos fleet, the MS *Elizabet Jung-Olsen*, a ship named after the grandmother of my young friend the late

Hermann. Born and brought up in a fishing station on the west coast of Jutland, a fisherman's wife to the end, daughter of Dogger Bank, Madame Elizabet had raised her son, Magnus, on a diet of nothing but seafood, and Hermann had often remembered her with warmth and respect in his letters to the journal.

But to my consternation, the mate was sitting over his dinner at the high table when I arrived, his wooden muse lying on the napkin in his lap. Apparently my fellow passengers could not bear to be deprived of his ridiculous "anecdotes." When he became aware of me the captain stood up, bowed briefly, and silently motioned me to sit at his side, but the rest were so absorbed in the story that they paid me no more attention than a puff of wind. Mate Caeneus did admittedly break off for a moment as I took my seat (this evening we were colleagues) but his silence might just as well have indicated a dramatic pause at a climactic moment of the story as the intention to show me any respect. I was rather hurt by this but as I had encountered a similar reception in the months immediately after the war, I preserved an impassive demeanor, clasped my hands on my stomach, and listened out of one ear. I kept the other tuned to the galley door, as it would soon be time for the fish stew.

Caeneus was describing the dealings of one of his shipmates, a man by the name of Polydeuces, with a full-grown monkey who belonged to the third woman he took on Lemnos:

"The woman used to dress the monkey in children's clothes and called it Thekkus after her former husband. It had been accustomed to having its mistress to itself for so long that when Polydeuces became a regular visitor to their bedchamber the animal went mad from jealousy and did everything in its power to persecute the interloper. The hero of the sea had to poleax the monkey every time he made love to the woman, or the creature would spring onto his back and try to tear out his jugular.

"In his battles with this shaggy, ill-tempered adversary, Polydeuces enjoyed the advantage of being one of the foremost boxers in the crew, as was subsequently revealed when we continued on our voyage and our way was blocked by Amicus, king of Brecia, who had the custom of knocking unconscious those who sought shelter from the winds in the bays of his land or went ashore there in search of water. As this was after Heracles had left us, Polydeuces volunteered to meet the king in single combat. Where King Amicus became maddened like a bull, Polydeuces, the son of Leda, was nimble as a swan's wing. So Polydeuces triumphed in his bouts with both Amicus and Thekkus, for it is precisely this combination of agility and strength that is required when subduing vicious monkeys."

The second mate continued with his story of a sailor who gets into fights with a monkey, a story that every mariner seems to have in his repertoire; why, I don't know. Perhaps it's an indication of the kind of audience they are used to? The present one was certainly amused—dear me, yes.

Caeneus went on:

"Perhaps you noticed that I said the monkey belonged to Polydeuces's third woman. For that is what she was, and only the third in a row of altogether twenty-seven sisters of Lemnos who made use of his manhood during the nine months or so that the Argonauts were guests in their land.

"Yes, after the revelry in the palace of Queen Hypsipyle had lasted the equivalent of a lunar month, we awoke one morning to find the court ladies armed and ordering us roughly to our feet with a loud clashing of weapons. We thought at first that this was a game, that they intended to incite us to perform morning feats of love by dressing up as battle-thirsty Amazons, but anyone who tried to grab a slim ankle or caress a soft buttock instantly had his blood let with the point of a spear. No, this was no game inspired by the goddess born of the foaming waves on the shores of Cyprus, this was in deadly earnest; our handmaidens had been transformed into shield maidens.

"To an accompaniment of harsh yells and evil threats from the women, we ordinary seamen of the many-nailed galley were forced to scramble to our feet and driven half-dressed and unwashed through the palace, through colonnades and passageways, right out beyond the encircling walls—and, please excuse my sailor's language:

"There we stood like idiots with our dicks in our hands.

"As we began to find our bearings a low growling rose from the men: How dare they treat heroes in such a manner? Could it be part of a greater and more dastardly plot? And what had become of Jason and those who remained in the palace? Had the perfidious termagants murdered them in their sleep and were they now planning to send us without captain or helmsman out onto the barren sea, where our ship would founder like an insignificant louse in the blue beard of mighty Poseidon?

"Thus the Argonauts grumbled to one another as they girded their loins and rubbed the sleep from their eyes or combed their tangled manes with their fingers. Our displeasure did not last long, however, for Jason now appeared on the balcony of Queen Hypsipyle's chamber and raised his hand, at which we fell silent.

"'Comrades, it may appear to you that the hospitality of Lemnos has faltered, but things are not as they seem. Our task here is far from over: behold!'

"He pointed to the city behind us.

"The troop turned and at first we could see nothing but the street up which we had marched so boldly only a few weeks before, which ran from the palace down the hill to the wealthier citizens' quarter, where it formed a gully between the houses and continued through the soldiers and artists' quarter to the marketplace, across the marketplace, and through the quarter of the artisans and common people, before winding through the paupers' quarter, after which it narrowed to an alley with hardly room to pass, known in everyday speech as She-wolf Alley—from where it was but a short walk down to the harbor and our vessel, the *Argo*. But even as the return route was revealed to us, we noticed a menacing movement in the shadows beside the gully mouth close by.

"Something huge and protean lurked there, something that seemed not to know whether to pounce or retreat—but was inclined to pounce. One moment its movements resembled a field of corn that sways in unison before the wind, the next it was chaotic, resembling nothing so much as an argument among the Hydra's seven quarreling heads. As we groped in vain for our weapons, we were reminded of our defenseless state: we would have to tackle this thing with our bare hands.

"Captain Jason, standing on the balcony with Queen Hypsipyle at his side, laughed provokingly and tapped his nose. Then, as if a spell had lifted from the crew of the *Argo*, our senses were unblocked and we smelled again the stench that our lovers in the palace had formerly emitted, only now it emanated from the creature confronting us. The veil was stripped from our eyes and we found ourselves faced with ninety desperate women lurking in the shade of one of the buildings.

"These were the finer ladies of Lemnos. They awaited us, silent and implacable—like the first steep hill in the path of a marathon runner."

•

When Mate Caeneus had finished, he shoveled down his food and went out to attend to his duties, while Captain Alfredson tapped his glass and announced to his fellow diners that now Mr. Haraldsson from Iceland was going to deliver an enlightening talk on an important topical issue. At these words the purser's lady friend made to rise from the table (on the pretext that she had to help her husband with the stocktaking), but the captain made it clear with a sharp glance that this could wait and she was to show me the courtesy of staying put during my edifying lecture. She obeyed, though in a put-upon manner. From looking at "her husband," the purser, more-over, we could tell that this fictional Wednesday evening stock count had taken him as much by surprise as the rest of us.

At coffee time the Norwegians had recommenced loading the ship and the work continued late into the evening, with the result that the machinery that inched the blocks of paper on board—cranes, winches, and windlass—now played first, second, and third fiddle to my talk, while the dockers' shouts and calls—"Heave ho! Easy now! Right! Left! Oi, you stupid bastard!"—formed my chorus.

Nevertheless, I began my lecture and immediately sensed that it was well received by those who had the wit to understand its content, although the speaker was rather put off his stride by the racket made by the loading crew. The talk itself was composed with consummate skill and delivered in the impeccable Danish characteristic of its author, though I say so myself. The fish stew, on the other hand, was a disaster. It was bland, contained far too little pepper, and instead of potatoes the cook had given in to his ridiculous whim of serving everything with rice. The resulting mixture was far from appetizing and formed a gray gloop on one's fork like spiky rice pudding.

In consequence, my little cultural contribution to life on board did not have quite the impact I had anticipated. It did not rise to the intended heights of *Gesamtkunstwerk*—to resort to a concept that had been familiar to me during my years on the Berlin radio.

FISH AND CULTURE

VI

"In its early stages the human heart resembles nothing so much as the heart of a fish. And there are numerous other factors that indicate our relationship to water-dwelling animals, were it no more than the fact that the human embryo has a gill arch, which alone would provide sufficient evidence that we can trace our ancestry back to aquatic organisms. The bone tissue of humans and animals consists of an organic solution, which when boiled produces a glue containing inorganic salts, principally calcium carbonate, but also composites of fluorine and magnesium. All these chemicals are found in solution in the sea, which is a further indication that land animals originally descended from sea creatures. The composition of blood also points the same way, for, as is well known, serious loss of blood can to a large extent be compensated for by using a 0.9 percent saline solution, while pure diluted seawater has been successfully employed for the same purpose. Finally, it seems highly probable that far from being descended from the same species of mammal as the other animals that share dry land with him, man has from the beginning represented a unique branch of the mammal family. Our teeth bear witness to this. They resemble neither the teeth of carnivores nor those of herbivores but are, on the contrary, designed to chew the sustenance provided by the sea. It may be concluded that some unknown entity in the warm prehistoric oceans developed into a fish, and that this fish evolved into a higher life-form that resembled man, which subsequently continued its development to become human (*Homo sapiens*). Let us therefore put forward the proposition that life colonized first the seas, then the land.

"It has been claimed that primitive man had his breeding grounds in the forests, a notion that has its basis in the ape theory, but as far as Europe is concerned, and particularly Scandinavia, one must disregard this hypothesis. The oldest human remains on the continent, found on the north coast of Spain and in France, are twenty thousand years old. There is every indication that these areas were home to a race of robust primitive men who shunned the forests and followed the coastline northward, while those who headed inland chose to dwell by rivers and lakes, where there was a prospect of fishing. The same was true of the aboriginal settlers of Scandinavia, who followed the edge of the ice sheet when the great glacier began to retreat at the waning of the Ice Age. Instead of following in the footsteps of the herbivores and the predators that preyed on them, they kept to the seashore, benefiting from the easy access to food.

"It would be superfluous to describe in detail the Nordic race's astonishing prowess in every field. People have observed with admiration the extraordinary vigor, stamina, and courage with which these relatively few dwellers of island and shore are endowed. There is a vast corpus of heroic tales devoted to their feats, from ancient days down to our own. They number in their thousands. We need only quote Claudius, who declared: 'They were proud of their height and looked down on the Romans for being so short.'

"The Nordic type is generally taller and more powerfully built than the German; the German from north Germany is more developed than the German from south Germany; the German from south Germany is taller than the Italian, and the northern Italians are more physically robust than their southern counterparts. Thus men's physical development diminishes the farther one moves from the northern coastal settlements and the more interbreeding there has been between coast- and mountain-dwellers. Right up until the beginning of the modern era, that is, the eighteenth century, communications between the upland and coastal districts all over Europe were fraught with difficulty. Coast-dwellers could travel by sea but otherwise were thrown back on their own resources, consuming what they caught for themselves. Likewise, the inhabitants of the inland districts had to subsist on what they could produce wherever they settled, hemmed in as they were by valley or moorland. The consumption of such different diets later resulted in the considerable disparity that now exists between the development and temperament of these two groups.

"As for miscegenation, suffice to mention here what the well-known Icelandic scholar Dr. Loftur Frodason writes of the inhabitants of Iceland's Trollaskagi peninsula: 'They are a race who dwell in isolation and have lived a peaceful life almost untouched by the outside world for centuries, without interbreeding with other people. They are a robust, naturally intelligent, and tall race. The men are handsome physical specimens, reminiscent of Bertel Thorvaldsen Gottskalkson's sculpture of Jason, with powerful barrel chests and slender hips. The women are no less exceptional in terms of dignity, carriage, and grace of movement.'

"That A. Cargill, mayor of Hull, had a similar view of these matters can be inferred from a talk he delivered to the Women's Luncheon Club in 1934, in which he pronounced the following opinion:

" 'Medical science is on the brink of proving once and for all that seafood is the healthiest diet available to man.'

"When men are prepared to declare so uncompromisingly that nutrients derived from the sea are essential to our health and boost both physical and mental development, one can hardly demur.

"The 'yellow peril' from the Far East lies in the innate energy and industriousness of the fish-eating nation of Japan. We can assume that the Japanese will swiftly overcome the problems resulting from the war, for they are endowed with the same qualities as the ancient Teutons who lived on the shores of Scandinavia yet conquered their way south to Rome and east to Constantinople. So we must ask ourselves: 'Would it not make sense for them to combine forces, these great fishing nations that dwell on opposite sides of the Earth?'

"When Rome declined, the emperors tried to resist the trend, thus Caesar Augustus summoned the Senate to compose a bill on the treatment of fish, while Nero equipped extravagant fishing fleets with nets of silk and lines of gold wire. Is this not a case of cause and effect? Where is Rome now?

"In conclusion, let us remember this:

"Life originates in the ocean and the ocean is the source from which life must seek its nourishment. The Nordic countries with their fish-rich coastal waters will continue to foster and rear vigorous generations, to the benefit of mankind; the Nordic countries have made a huge contribution to world culture (both with regard to their racial qualities and their inventions—everything from the steam engine and electricity to the airplane and wireless); the Nordic countries are mighty—the might of the sea is boundless.

"The sea is the mainspring of the Nordic nations!"

Lecture delivered to the crew of the
MS Elizabet Jung-Olsen, *April 13, 1949*

MORE LIFE ON
THE OCEAN WAVE

VII

Nothing stirs; there is not a soul to be seen above deck, on ship or wharf. Even the wagons, hanging at regular intervals as far as the eye can see, to the very top of the mountain, rock noiselessly on their cable. Today is a day of no work, for today marks the beginning of the Easter holiday and the locals' rules on holidays are nonnegotiable. A Norwegian who works on an important religious festival will go straight to parboil in hell. So much was to be gathered from the words of Raguel Bastesen's deputy, who this morning made radio contact from Stavanger with the news that the loading would not be completed until the evening of the Tuesday after Easter. Unfortunately, in all the commotion following the accident they had neglected to inform Captain Alfredson of this fact. It was to be understood from the man's words that we should not be taking it for granted that he should even pass on this bad news to us on a Shrove Tuesday, since, strictly speaking, all such radio communications counted as work and his future place in heaven was now in grave jeopardy.

We had to resign ourselves to this state of affairs, though some felt it put rather a damper on things to be forced to twiddle their fingers in this dreary spot for another five whole days. The Norwegian tried to console us by pointing out the beauty of the scenery just over the mountains. He suggested we do some sightseeing, go on a few excursions, join the cargo steamer that went at regular intervals to the small towns farther up the fjord, from where one could take scheduled buses up the valleys and there go skiing and amuse ourselves in the evenings with dancing and singing; there was really no excuse to be bored. Although it was some comfort for the crew to hear this from such a well-informed local, it was little consolation for me, as I had planned to spend my vacation in the Mediterranean and Black Sea, not Norway's Vest-Agder.

It was reported that Director Bastesen had arrived in Oslo accompanied by a nurse, and that from there he had booked a cruise to the West Indies to recuperate from the blow to his head—all at the expense of the paper mill.

The cruise ship was due to leave that evening.

And the man called himself a social democrat!

•

After lunch I ran into Captain Alfredson on deck and remarked in a jocular tone:

"So the Great Cham is exiled from Fedafjord . . ."

He asked me in return if I would like to accompany him, the first mate, the purser, and his lady friend to the nearest town. It was an approximately two-hour journey, partly by motorboat, partly by automobile. I thanked him kindly for the invitation but said I would wait to hear how they got on.

When the party returned at dinnertime the purser told me that the landscape they traveled through had been very picturesque but the "town" itself was small and everything had been closed, so it wasn't really much of an outing. However, they had taken part in a Norwegian holiday luncheon at a ski hut. Apparently it had been first-rate fare, mostly meat but they had also been offered the princess of the seas: herring, no less.

The purser's lady friend on the other hand had found their trip a hair-raising experience and had apparently been scared out of her wits for most of the way. I overheard her complaining to the cook, describing how the first mate had driven at breakneck speed along precipitous mountain roads with the sea a thousand feet below, and claiming that she never wanted to set foot on Norwegian soil again. After this the woman sighed, rested her hand on the cook's shoulder, and laid her head on his breast.

Oho, I thought as I watched them unobserved from the galley door that stood open into the saloon. But the cook laid his hand between the woman's shoulder blades, simultaneously moving backward, while she took what looked like a clumsy dance step past him to the kitchen sink, where she proceeded to throw up into the potato pan, which was sitting there waiting to be washed up by the galley hand.

From the ship one can glimpse a road clinging to the mountain on the other side of the fjord. It runs diagonally up the slope and for a long stretch appears to be little more than a ledge on the sheer rock wall, so it seemed only natural to me that the woman should have been carsick after being driven along it at breakneck speed.

But still I thought:

Oho . . .

•

"Looks like it's only the two of you this evening."

With a deft swivel of the wrist the steward placed the dish containing the entrée on the table and began to serve it onto our plates.

"The first mate is on watch. The others are exhausted after their trip and say they're still stuffed with Norwegian food. You two could stay here till the early hours and enjoy the same meal three times over . . ."

He laughed at his own joke, as young men will. Although I did not join in, I indicated by my response that I found his cheeriness far from unwelcome. It was the first sign of life in the saloon that Shrove Tuesday evening in Mold Bay. We two—Mate Caeneus and I—had been sitting there waiting for the others without saying a single word beyond the conventional greetings. He was, in fact, as taciturn as the day we met on deck (though I have to admit that his clean, pressed uniform lent the occasion a silent dignity).

However, I felt the steward's fooling had gone far enough so I raised my brows and gestured to the center of the table:

"In that case, would it not be more appropriate for us to sit there?"

The steward and mate looked at me inquiringly. I moved my hand slightly to the left, just enough to indicate the empty seat at my side:

"In Captain Alfredson's absence."

"Oh, that's what you're driving at!"

"Yes, he is our host, is he not?"

"Well, of course . . ."

I need hardly explain that this exchange was with the steward since my dining companion remained persistently mute. I lost my temper with the young man:

"You have still not deigned to inform us why the commanding officer's seat is unoccupied this evening."

"Oh, I, er, he was . . ."

"That is no concern of ours!"

I gave the table a sharp rap with my index finger. The steward flinched from the blow as if I had struck him.

"You cannot evade your duties by gossiping about your superior officer!"

The steward rolled his eyes like a negro, stammering something incomprehensible in his Fynen dialect. At this point Mate Caeneus spoke up:

"What Mr. Haraldsson means—with respect, sir— is that it's not at all clear who has the role of host this evening. Isn't that so, Mr. Haraldsson?"

I nodded to the mate, who looked the boy straight in the eye, his expression stern:

"You should of course have begun by bidding me good evening first and then Mr. Haraldsson. That would have made it clear from the start that in the absence of Captain Alfredson and the first mate, I stand in the place of host."

The tip of the steward's tongue protruded from between his dry lips:

"Thank you, Caeneus, sir, thank you, Second Mate. I shall remember that next time, thank you, thank you . . ."

He approached the table, gabbling his thanks and fumbling with a shaking hand for the crystal carafe, presumably with a view to pouring our wine. But Mate Caeneus was quicker off the mark. He hastily removed the stopper from the carafe and, softening his voice a little, said to the boy:

"That'll do for the time being. Go into the galley and take a look at the book of etiquette. Then you'll do better with the main course."

To me he said politely:

"May I offer you a glass of bittersweet Alsace wine with your ham, Mr. Haraldsson?"

I accepted his offer. By establishing our respective roles at the Shrove Tuesday dinner, I had succeeded in breaking the ice between Mate Caeneus and myself. He poured my wine with a more cosmopolitan air than one would expect of a seaman, filling only a third of the glass. Then he poured one for himself and invited me please to start.

I waited until the galley door had closed behind the steward, then whispered to my new host:

"Mark my words, there'll be something other than potatoes with tonight's main course . . ."

"Is that so . . . ?" he replied.

I said no more.

•

The evening passed swiftly—without any further gaffes by the boy—in amicable chat about the events of the past few days, and before I knew it we had reached the brandy, and the cigars, which I still could not accept. Ordinarily Mate Caeneus would embark on his tale at this stage, but as I couldn't bear the thought of having to listen to him relating the next chapter for me alone, then listening to him repeat it all to the other crew members the following day, I had the brainwave of asking him about something that intrigued me, and was moreover connected to his story:

"I should be fascinated, Mr. Mate, to hear you relate the story of the prop, if I may call it that, which you use for your storytelling."

Thus I gave the appearance of taking an interest in my obsessive dining companion, who by virtue of his role as host was the highest-ranking officer on board the MS *Elizabet Jung-Olsen* that evening.

"Ah, that . . ." he said, obviously pleased that I had provided him with an opportunity to discourse at length about himself. He reached into the inside pocket of his uniform jacket and took out the piece of wood:

"This is a splinter from the bow timber of the *Argo*."

He balanced the splinter on his palm carefully, as if the slightest draft could blow it away, and held it up to the candlelight to give me a better view. The stick looked like nothing so much as a piece of rotten driftwood of the type that used to wash up on the shore in my youth: bored by worms, gnawed by insects, polished by wind and water, hammered by rocks. I leaned forward and sniffed the wood: nothing. Or was there? Yes, there was a faint tang of salt mingled with the odor of damp soil. And to my astonishment I became aware of a once-familiar stirring in a certain part of my anatomy, in the nether regions, so to speak:

Good gracious me! I thought, dropping the napkin over my lap and straightening up in my chair:

"But how does it work?"

The mate withdrew his hand and raised the piece of wood to his right ear:

"You've seen me listening to it, sir . . ."

He made an amateurish pretense of listening to the wood chip:

"I hear something that could best be compared with the soporific hiss of our shortwave radio receiver: as if a handful of golden sand were being shaken in a fine sieve. This sound caresses the eardrum so gently that before you know it your ear has been lulled to sleep. Then I hear a faint humming through the hiss. At first I think I'm mistaken, but no, I hear it again—rising and falling, over and over, unvarying.

"Once the ear has fallen asleep, the humming takes on a new form. It becomes a note, a voice sounding in the consciousness, as if a single grain of golden sand had slipped through the mesh of the sieve and, borne on the tip of the eardrum's tongue, passed through the horn and ivory-inlaid gates that divide the tangible from the invisible world.

"At first it is wordless, like crooning over a cradle, then it swells into a song. The singer is a woman."

"Now, there's a surprise . . ." I remarked rather loudly, inadvertently interrupting Mate Caeneus.

"I beg your pardon?"

"Never mind . . ." I answered, adding, "I think the pork chops must have disagreed with me."

While the mate droned on about his piece of wood, I wondered whether oak trees had genders and whether the reason for the unexpected response in my nether regions to the smell of the splinter was that it had been split off a female tree.

"As you will remember, sir, Athena fitted the bow timber into the many-nailed *Argo* and the nature of her gift was such that it had the power of human speech. Without it we would never have found our way through the Bosphorus, across the Black Sea to Colchis, up the Danulse and her tributaries, into the Baltic and the North Sea, and from there north across the Atlantic to cruise off the chill island of Thule, that strange land shrouded in eternal darkness, where the water boils of its own accord in the snow. Indeed, it was on the black sands of Ultima Thule that we Argonauts, first of mortal men, saw the gleam of Helios's harp strings as he dwells with the Hyperboreans and tunes his instrument beneath the vault of the world. Without the guidance of the loquacious oak we would not have known to turn our ship south-southeast and thus find the way home to the civilized world of the Mediterranean.

"After this journey we mortal men had somewhat humbled the pride of blue-haired Poseidon, for by our successful voyage one could say that we Argonauts had conquered great territories in his watery realm."

"Excuse me . . ."

Here I raised a finger:

"Pray excuse me, good host, I have to go and spend a penny."

Mate Caeneus:

"Of course . . ."

I hurried to the lavatory and relieved myself. "He" was perhaps not quite as sprightly as the last time this fit was upon him—but he was lively enough. Yes, it gladdened my old heart to see how much vigor the scent of the precious speaking wood had injected into the "old chap."

·

When I returned to the saloon I noticed that Caeneus had refilled our brandy glasses. His glass, that is to say, for I myself had been sipping my drink sparingly—not wishing to abuse Magnus Jung-Olsen's hospitality—whereas the mate was becoming a little the worse for wear.

I sat down beside him without comment, then ventured to suggest something that had occurred to me in the lavatory:

"I was thinking: Could the voice you detect in the humming of the wood be your own voice? Like the poet who obstinately believes that he is writing about the world but is in reality only telling yet another story about himself?"

The idea was not entirely my own. My brother-in-law, the psychiatrist Dr. Pázmány, had said something similar when the invisible people moved in with me during the winter of 1910–11. However, Mate Caeneus's response to this little theory of mine—which was only a friendly suggestion—was to scowl and pout and rest his cheek on his hand while his black eyes stared into space.

A good while passed in this manner. I kept silence with him, and it didn't occur to me to try to explain my words or elaborate. I was becoming used to the crew members' tendency to behave as if everything I said was incomprehensible, to remain silent for just as long as I was speaking, then carry on from where they had left off, treating me like some guano-covered rock that one must steer a course around. While we two sat in silence over our brandy glasses, I amused myself by trying to work out what the mate was staring at—no doubt he would soon take up the thread from where he had left off when I slipped out to answer the call of nature. It seemed to me that his gaze was resting halfway between the teaspoon and the crumb of French bread just above the middle of the table, a little to the right from his point of view.

But, as it happened, the mate did not yield, any more than a chess piece that has already been played. I had, so to speak, the floor. The clock was ticking on my side. But instead of following up my previous comment by stating the obvious: "when your gaze is so abstracted that you seem to see beyond field and forest, you are in fact staring at what stands closest to you; yourself," courtesy bade me say:

"Has this awe-inspiring object been in your possession long?"

Mate Caeneus's large, curly head lifted from his hand. He looked at me inquiringly. To my horror I saw that his left eye, which had been resting on his palm, was full of tears. He cleared his throat and answered as if from the dregs of sleep:

"You read my thoughts, sir. I was just recalling the terrible night I acquired this talkative stick."

The mate seized his brandy glass from the table, raised it to face level, and looked over the brim—straight into my eyes:

"Your health, shipmate Haraldsson!"

The saloon clock struck twelve.

VIII

By the end I was having difficulty following the plot, both because the storyteller's words had become slurred with drink and because my own head was nodding. But so much is certain: the mate told me that one night, long after the Argonauts had returned home with the Golden Fleece, he was down on the waterfront in the city of Corinth. The weather was bad and there were few people abroad apart from Caeneus himself and his companions, a few squawking herring gulls, and a clutch of adolescent kittens that he stressed had been both ill-favored and irksome. By this stage in the story the hero's world had suffered such an ill wind that his errand to the boat shed was to scavenge for something to eat. There he could usually find fish guts left over from the day's catch, rotting crustaceans and dubious scallops, if his luck was in.

And would you know it? This time the easily pleased protagonist spotted a basket of bait that had somehow rolled over and was propped up on its side in the lee of a blue-and-white-striped fishing boat, while the shark bait—consisting mainly of mares' intestines—lay wet and inviting in the sand. Caeneus glided into the shade and began to bolt down this feast in frenzied rivalry with the other gulls (his words), and the rapture of the competitive glut was so all-consuming that Caeneus couldn't tear himself away from the delicacies even when an unseen bird-catcher jerked a string that was buried in the sand and tied to the end of the twig propping up the basket. The swarm of gulls whirled from under the keel of the boat like a foaming wave and Caeneus felt like the luckiest dog alive to be left alone with the mares' bowels in the darkness of the basket.

The bird-catcher soon put an end to the fun, however. He stuck his hairy human hand under the bait basket, seized the feather-soft bird's neck he encountered there, and extracted Caeneus, who realized belatedly that he had walked into a trap.

Caeneus fought viciously with the hunter, pecking at his hands with his strong yellow beak, beating his head with silver-gray wings, and clawing his chest with pink, fleshless feet, but the hunter tightened his hold on his prey, whirling Caeneus around hard in the hope of breaking his neck. It was an unequal struggle. The god of heaven had granted Caeneus the power of imperviousness to weapons and fists whereas the bird-catcher was the most wretched of vagabonds: a bald, haggard, pinch-bellied, shrunken-limbed old man—and as such was bound to yield to the bird in the end. But just as the bird-catcher loosened his grip and Caeneus squirmed from his hands, their eyes met:

"Oh no . . ."

Grief crushed the liver-red gull's heart as Caeneus recognized in the tramp's burst pupils the most splendid champion the world had ever known, the man who had commanded the most famous heroes in days of yore, he who had won the love of queens and enchantresses; yes, there the gull saw the ruins of his old captain, Jason son of Aeson.

Caeneus shrank away from this terrible revelation. He called Jason's name, called his own name, called on Hermes to free his tongue from its fetters, but all the son of Aeson could see and hear was a herring gull squawking on a rock. Caeneus craned his neck, cocked his head back, and screeched:

"Arrk, arrk! Ga-ga-ga-ga! Arrk, arrk . . ."

The graybeard Jason fled down the beach and the fleet-winged Caeneus took to the air in pursuit. Although stones harmed him no more than spears or knuckles, it took energy and concentration to dodge the pebbles that Jason was throwing in his direction, and Caeneus was worn out from the fight. So he hovered at a safe height above the knock-kneed man as he ran and crawled away over the sand. But soon hunger overcame fear and Jason began to search for something else to eat; at least the crazed herring gull seemed to have stopped trying to peck him. When the decrepit hero of the seas had scraped together enough for his supper he sought somewhere safe to eat it, in peace from other vagabonds, wild dogs, and rats. He found sanctuary in the fabled graveyard of ships.

Here the sea castles of yesteryear lay rotting like beached whales on the sand, their timbers brittle, ropes rotten, nails rusty, the black and red paint that had adorned them from gunwale to keel quite worn away. Jason found a place by the prow of one of the many-nailed hulks and began to gorge himself in frantic haste, with constantly darting eyes. Once the meal was over he leaned against the ship's hull, took a deep breath, and sighed as happily as after a banquet of old.

At that the splendid timberwork behind him creaked as if the rotten ship were groaning.

Then he heard a voice say:

"Jason? Is that you?"

The voice was hollow and cracked, yet so powerful that it fluttered the tramp's white beard. With a shriek of terror Jason flung himself on all fours and peered around in search of the foe. The voice continued:

"O Jason, have you come to take me away?"

Jason spun around on his knuckles and yelped:

"What? Where are you? Come out if you dare!"

"Lord, I have awaited your coming ever since we landed at the city of Iolcus, when the harbor resounded with the cheers of the welcoming multitude for thrice nine days and nights, when the precious wine overflowed my thwarts from bow to stern, when the leafy olive branch wound up my mast, when the perfume of the vestal virgins' incense wafted over my yards and rigging—when you disembarked, never to return."

For, you see, Caeneus and Jason were not the only members of the famous quest for the golden ram's fleece to be present in Corinth that night. That many-nailed masterpiece, the *Argo*, was there as well. She it was who lay there in the ships' graveyard, gnawed through by the teeth of time, lamenting so plaintively:

"Take me away. Sail me out to sea, the blue sea, where Poseidon shakes his trident at bold seafarers who steer their ships through the mountainous waves as if they were thunderbolts from the hand of supreme Zeus."

But Jason recognized neither the galley nor her voice, and it made no difference how softly she cajoled her old captain:

"Oh, how I have missed the feel of your strong feet walking my decks . . ."

He merely raged in the sand like a fighting cur, and when the enemy failed to show itself he rolled over on his back and began to howl and lament—sure that madness had taken hold of him.

Caeneus, who had observed the whole scene from his vantage point in the sky, now arrived on silent wings and perched on the *Argo* where the bowsprit met the prow.

The weary old ship creaked:

"Caeneus?"

"ARRK! ARRK! ARRK!"

The gull squawked and flapped its wings as the bow timber gave way with a groan of pain and fell to the ground, crushing the man beneath.

And that was the end of Jason son of Aeson.

But Corinth was not the end of the road for the herring gull Caeneus. He flew away, bearing in his claws a splinter of wood from the bow timber, which he has used for his storytelling ever since. Feeling things had become too hot for him in the Aegean, he persisted in his flight until he came all the way north to Finnmark. There a shaman took him under his wing and turned him back into the likeness of a man.

He had stayed a long time in the land of the Lapps, and since then had always worked on Scandinavian ships, generally as mate but occasionally as a telegraphist.

So Caeneus maundered on until the early hours. I must have fallen asleep in my chair and been carried by him to my quarters. I have no memory of undressing myself—it must have been him because my clothes were not in the cupboard but lay on the desk chair, though everything was neatly folded and the shirt and jacket had been hung over the back. This is still further proof that he had been well brought up, in spite of his interminable verbal diarrhea.

I slept until three o'clock in the afternoon.

Today is Good Friday.

Need I say more?

•

In an attempt to make the day of crucifixion bearable for us, Captain Alfredson ordered a more lavish spread than usual, so we would have all the ingredients for a feast, as far as circumstances allowed. As the evening progressed the guests grew merry, and the captain was not behind-hand in ensuring that everyone had a thoroughly good time. People told jokes which frequently raised a smile, and many of them were well received, though others were not quite as adept at finding the words for what they wished to say, and there were those who verged on the risqué. But, on the whole, one cannot deny that the evening was most congenial.

The purser's lady friend, who seemed to have an absolute monopoly over the serving of alcoholic beverages, was now in the best of spirits and I could see no sign that she harbored a grudge against me. She served us liberally, filling her neighbors' glasses and asking the diners please not to be shy about helping one another to wine. In fact, as it turned out, everyone had rather more than they wished for. What reason she had to play both host and hostess that evening and offer the drink so freely I cannot say, though I have a hunch that as ever the couple's addiction to profit was to the fore, since I had gathered from Captain Alfredson that my hospitality bill, like those of the officers, would be paid by the shipping company, however high. So the couple would profit from any refreshments we consumed over and above what was considered a normal part of the meals, and alcohol weighed heavily in the balance. I tried to raise the matter with Alfredson but the woman saw and forestalled me by rising from her seat and inviting the guests to drink a toast to the captain, which we did with a good will.

Pleased as punch, Alfredson hurried to his quarters and returned with a stack of records and a gramophone. Seeing this, the first mate grabbed the corners of the tablecloth, one after another, and whipped it off the table complete with all the dishes and the remains of the rum trifle. He swung it over his shoulder like a sailor's kit bag, swept into the galley, and flung it in the corner with a resounding crash and clatter of breaking crockery. I saw the purser's lady friend laugh out loud at this, for the purser could also charge the shipping line for loss of tableware. The captain slammed the gramophone down on the table and the second engineer was set to winding it up and choosing the music; drinking songs, as it turned out—tales of womanizing and debauchery in thirteen languages.

The instant the needle touched the groove in the record the purser's lady friend became the focus of the party. Everyone had to dance with her in turn: the captain, the first engineer, first mate, cook, steward, and the three deckhands who were off duty—it was Cae-neus's watch—while I myself filled in for the second engineer and twirled the gramophone crank while he twirled the woman.

From where I sat, squeezed up against the phono-graph, I couldn't block my ears to song after song de-scribing the sailor's life. The most memorable for me was a comic number listing all the scrapes that drinkers can get into:

> I went to Australia and there I was happy:
> I bought dozens of girls for a month at a time.
> I went down to Italy and there I was happy:
> I poleaxed the barmen who didn't serve me on
>   time.
> I went to Rhodesia and there I was happy:
> I knocked down wry-faced old blackamoors with
>   my fists of steel.
> I went to Colombia and there I was happy:
> I took married women to my bed and enjoyed
>   them for a while.
>   (Retold in my own words, V. H.)

The chorus went as follows:

> I ended up in hell and here I am happy.
> And I have this to say to anyone who's curious
>   about my lot:

I feel no compunction for what I have done.
I have no interest in the dishonored—
No interest in the dead.

(Retold in my own words, V. H.)

Why should this particular song have been etched in my memory so that I can record its contents here? Well, because during the last verse the purser's lady friend came dancing up to me with one of the Kronos line's fine linen napkins in her hand. She had folded the napkin into a Napoleon hat. As the woman bent forward to place the hat on my head, my senses were filled with a powerful odor of mingled gin, cigarettes, eau de cologne, hair spray, and sweat—before she straightened up and screeched:

"*Du bist doch mein süßer Papageientaucher . . .*"

I laughed at this along with the rest while thinking to myself that Dr. Pázmány would have been able to read a thing or two from the woman's behavior, especially when she called me "her puffin."

Be that as it may, when the carousing was at its height and the music had begun to pierce one's ears like the song of the sirens, I heard someone shouting above the din of the gramophone:

"Hey, hey there! I . . . you! Listen, hey, listen! Hey, you!"

The purser was standing apart from the milling throng, snatching at his shipmates, one after the other, in an attempt to buttonhole them. He was one of those whom Bacchus renders eloquent, and had imbibed just the right dose of spirits to fine-tune his speech organ to the point where his inability to pronounce his "r"s had largely disappeared. This emboldened him to make pronouncements, and he began imparting loudly into my right ear everything that he had on his chest—I was his sole audience and confidant once his shipmates on the dance floor had shaken him off—and unfortunately it has to be said that it was pretty poor, thin stuff, though it contained the odd interesting tidbit.

Including the news that he had purchased his lady friend for the price of a leg of pork:

THE PURSER'S TALE

There is a type of venomous snake known as *Vipera ursini*. It is about a foot and a half long, ash-gray with brown spots and prominent black markings that zigzag the length of its spine. This snake lives in the undergrowth on the forest floor, devouring small animals, both hot- and cold-blooded, though it will sometimes undertake long forays into areas inhabited by man. Here it suddenly appears, having slithered under tree roots, down streams, along tracks, and across the borders of the wood, all the way to the dark green thicket of willow that stands on the eastern edge of the old garden on the

Polish estate of Tz—, posing as a compromise between cultivated land and untouched nature.

In late summer these willow shrubs provide the shadiest place in the garden and the *Gouvernante* was in the habit of taking her little charges there to amuse themselves; the *Gouvernante* being the governess who looked after the grandchildren of the elderly aristocrat and former magistrate, Tz—. He was a widower and usually lived alone apart from his servants, but because of the war, his daughter-in-law and her three children had come to stay with him while their father was away directing the defense of the homeland. One day, following afternoon tea, the *Gouvernante* appeared in the shade of the shrubbery with the baby Opheltes, the long-awaited son, in her arms. She led the younger girl by the hand while the elder ran off at a tangent with her butterfly net aloft, trying to capture the mayflies that glowed bewildered in the sunshine.

The *Gouvernante* had no sooner reached the thicket of rough willow shrub than out of it stepped seven heavily armed men. They were equipped for a secret mission, in black overalls and lace-up leather boots, with provisions in knapsacks and their faces painted camouflage green. The woman didn't spot them until they parted the leafy branches and materialized before her. Upon which she gave a scream of terror and was about to flee with the children when the leader of the gang spoke:

"You see before you friends of the fatherland; we mean you no harm."

He raised his hands and showed her that they were empty. And the woman thought to herself, those are the hands of an artisan—they offer me no threat. The others also raised their hands. And their leader continued:

"All we want is something to drink, then we'll be on our way: our business is with the Germans at the fortress of Thebes."

She answered:

"I can give you water. Come with me to the house, where you'll be given both food and drink . . ."

"Thank you, good woman, but our mission is secret and we cannot afford to lose any time. So we'll continue on our way."

He signaled to his men to turn back into the forest and they began to part the branches of the willow, preparing to vanish into the thicket again, but the woman said:

"Wait! There's a well nearby that's used to water the horses when they're grazing here in the old garden. The water's fresh and full of invigorating minerals, since Mr. Tz— loves his riding horses as if they were his own children."

The man answered:

"The Polish steed is a divine creature. What is good enough for him is good enough for us."

"Then I'll show you the way."

But because the well could not be seen from where they stood and the *Gouvernante* wanted Opheltes to enjoy the sunshine in the lee of the willows, she laid him on the grass and told his sisters to keep an eye on their little brother for the brief time it would take her to escort the men to within sight of the well. The boy had just learned to crawl, and the moment his nurse turned her back on him he rolled over on his stomach and crawled laughing under a bush where *Vipera ursini* was waiting.

Although the venom of this European species of viper is not powerful enough to kill an adult, it brings certain death to any toddler it bites—and when the *Gouvernante* returned to the sheltered spot, only a minute later, the little child Opheltes Tz— lay dead in a tangle of willow roots, and the snake had vanished.

When the thirsty friends of the fatherland saw the tragedy that had taken place, their leader said:

"This is an ill omen for our expedition, and the boy's true name should be Arkemoros: 'Harbinger of Ruin.'"

Sure enough, all seven of them lost their lives in the attack on the fortress at Thebes.

The Tz— family nursed their vengeance until the end of the war, though they compelled the guilt-stricken *Gouvernante* to serve them in every conceivable manner in the meantime. Afterward they handed her over to a

Soviet tank platoon that came raping and pillaging through the region.

Four years later the purser found the woman in a whorehouse in Königsberg. The day before, he had acquired a leg of dried ham, and in exchange for this he was allowed to take the woman away with him.

IX

I should think today, Saturday, April 16, has been the most remarkable of the voyage so far. From early this morning till late this evening we have experienced one novelty after another. On the dot of six the rumbling and clanking began as every machine and winch on deck, fore and aft, ground into action as the loading was resumed with urgent haste. There was little chance of sleeping while this was going on so I got out of bed.

I put on my dressing gown and went out into the saloon, where I found the crew, who had been dragged out of bed so that the loading of the ship could progress with all speed. Although the industriousness of the Norwegian dockers should have been cause for optimism, there was a subdued atmosphere among the deckhands at the breakfast table. Not that this was surprising. Many of them had caroused until nearly two in the morning and inevitably some had continued in their cabins, a few passing out in their bunks with a bottle tucked under their cheek—not that it bothered me.

What did come as a surprise was that the purser's lady friend should say good morning to me. She seemed to do so on impulse, quite cheerfully. I returned the greeting drily, though with perfect civility, and waited all through breakfast for the sting in the tail. But no, she merely finished her breakfast, took her leave of me in the same amiable manner, and went off to start her chores; she had to work for two that day for, as she put it wittily, the purser was working in bed.

I was still scratching my head over the woman's change of heart when the first engineer accosted me and invited me to go skiing with him. He had borrowed a car and planned to drive an hour or so up a fairly long valley to a place with ski slopes and a winter hotel for wealthy guests. There I would have a chance to try out something new, especially with regard to ski runs, with which he assumed I was little acquainted. He was sure we would be given a royal welcome at the hotel and had booked a table so we could lunch with the thirty other guests who were staying there. We could expect to sit down to eat with stockbrokers and politicians from Sweden and Norway, not to mention industrialists, ski jumpers, actresses, and shipping tycoons.

I patted the engineer on the shoulder, saying it was a kind invitation and a kind thought on the part of a fit young man to an old-timer, but unfortunately I didn't feel I could accept. I was here as a guest of my benefactor Magnus Jung-Olsen and did not wish to abuse his hospitality by preferring a Norwegian ski hut to the fine amenities offered by the flagship of the Kronos line.

The engineer said he perfectly understood; he himself had never before sailed on such a well-appointed ship as the MS *Elizabet Jung-Olsen*, although he couldn't boast such princely quarters as I, who lodged in two spacious cabins with an en suite bathroom. And with that we parted company.

•

All afternoon I watched the loading of the ship. It was an impressive sight as the white blocks of raw paper came swooping over the ship like banks of cloud before descending with a loud whine into the hold. A young person would no doubt find this pastime a touch monotonous but I managed to see something new in every block. I watched the loading from various angles thanks to the solicitude of the deckhands, who shifted me hither and thither around the deck so I wouldn't be in any danger. There I stayed until the first mate came over and asked whether I would like to be his guest on the bridge, which afforded a good view of the operations, saying he would also like to take this chance to introduce me to the innovations in navigation equipment that were to be seen there, for at this point wartime inventions had begun to flood onto the general market—to the benefit of us all.

Yes, the ship was certainly well equipped and there had been many innovations since I rowed out to the fishing grounds with my father seventy years ago. The mate's seat, for example, was a leather upholstered armchair, which could be tilted back and forth, spun in a circle, or raised and lowered at will. Then there was the gallon-capacity coffee machine, divided into two compartments, which could also hold hot water for tea. It was bolted on to a waist-high hardwood cupboard in one corner of the wheelhouse, and set into the worktop beside it was a pewter tin full of English shortbread. The first engineer invited me to sit in the armchair, then brought me coffee and shortbread on a tray that he clipped to the right arm of the chair. And before leaving to attend to his duties he handed me a pair of binoculars and turned on the wireless: "Turalleri," "Pumpa lens," and "Hut la ti tei"—Norwegian sailors' ditties performed in poignant and heartfelt style by the much-loved Magnus Samuelsen.

However, the greatest pleasure for me was to see the blocks of raw paper gliding past the wheelhouse windows. Now that I was on a level with them I could see how far the raw product fell short of the quality book paper that was shortly destined to preserve the words of the Prophet or the speeches of Atatürk. With the help of the binoculars I could distinguish the discoloration of the half-worked pulp, for although the blocks had appeared snow-white from a distance, I now saw that they were shot through with bark-colored fibers that sometimes had a greenish tinge. The best opportunity to examine this came when the workmen in the hold failed to keep up with their counterparts on shore, for then the block would stop swaying and hang still for a decent interval before my eyes.

On one such occasion I spotted something unexpected: one of the deceased workman's hands was trapped in the outer layer of the paper pulp. The little finger and half the ring finger were missing but a wedding band still encircled the stub, and the bones were visible through a gaping wound in the palm.

Before I could alert the workers, the block was lowered into the hold and I thought to myself that it would be a hopeless task to find the hand in the gloom below. So I decided to keep the knowledge to myself; the crew were superstitious enough as it was. And even I had my doubts that fortune would favor any ship that carried a dead man's hand.

Indeed, I had grave doubts on this score.

•

Mate Caeneus listened for an unusually long time to his wood chip that Saturday evening in Mold Bay. For, as it transpired, it had some peculiar things to impart. Certainly Caeneus was frowning when he lowered the chip from his ear and replaced it in the inside pocket of his officer's jacket. He drained his coffee cup at one go, wiped his mouth with the back of his hand, and said in a low voice:

"When I began my account of the Argonauts' sojourn in the realm of doe-eyed Hypsipyle, I told you that we sailors got into some tight spots at times, and once I only narrowly avoided killing myself through sheer recklessness—during our shore leave on Lemnos, as it happens.

"After more than three months on the island a few of us younger deckhands had the bright idea of organizing a race in the chariots left behind by our mistresses' former husbands. These were solidly built, showy vehicles, inlaid with gold leaf and engraved with images of the swiftest-flying gods and fabulous creatures of antiquity: wing-footed Hermes, rosy-fingered Eos, Pegasus of the shining mane, and shimmering Iris—all sprinting hell-for-leather across the wide fields of heaven.

"My mistress at the time was called Iphenoa. She was in her thirties and had been married to a lieutenant, for by this point in time the crew of the *Argo* had finished with the smartest district of the town and we were now servicing the needs of the women in the soldiers and artists' quarter. Iphenoa had two nubile daughters. On the day of the race she accompanied me to the starting line and knotted a blue brocade scarf around my neck for luck. Her daughters harnessed the racehorses to the chariot, referring to one as Cat and the other as Death. These were giant beasts that the poets would have described as snorting fireworks, for Cat was of the same stock as Bucephalos, Alexander the Great's steed, with toes instead of hooves, while Death was gray, with eyes of blue.

"During the weeks I had spent in the women's home, both sisters had tried in turn to entice me into bed, but unlike many of my shipmates I refused to serve more than one woman from each family, and never young girls. The maidservants were another matter—and here the daughters felt I was rubbing salt in the wound—for I was quite willing to roger the servants when the mistress was away from home. So I should have been on my guard. When Iphenoa had kissed me on the mouth and was leading the lieutenant's daughters to the stands, the girls glanced back over their shoulders, smiling at me most oddly.

"We raced five at a time, and in the second heat my fellow charioteers consisted of Peleus, father of Achilles; Acastus, son of Pelias; Staphylus 'bunch of grapes,' son of Dionysus; and the huntress Atalanta.

"The latter competed on behalf of those celibates who took no part in the womanizing but remained on board the *Argo* and guarded the ship under the command of Heracles.

"The judge raised his arm. He let it fall.

"The horses leaped into action. The charioteers yelled.

"Then the sky was blue over Lemnos. Then the waves lapped the shore, then the limestone threw back the sunlight and the men's skin shone until they seemed as insubstantial as immortals. Everything sang to the same tune; no ear could distinguish among the hoof-beats, the creaking of the wheels, and the shouts of the charioteers.

"Half an eternity passed in this manner.

"I had driven no more than ninety feet when the spokes in the left wheel of my chariot gave way. As if by a miracle, Cat and Death broke free from the yoke and suffered no harm, but the chariot and ground collided with such colossal force that all I can remember is being hurled into the air in a forward trajectory and landing on the undercarriage, where I danced a brief tarantella before everything went black.

"When I came to my senses Jason was standing over me, looking very grave. He said I had broken both my legs. I'm told that I smiled back at him as if it were nothing to make a fuss about. Then I swooned again and had no idea that my life was hanging by a thread. Next I woke to discover that my clothes were being cut off, and I was vaguely aware of a girl drawing splinters of wood from my chest, for which I was grateful. But when the wounds were stitched up without an anesthetic, the pain was so great that I blacked out. I must have surfaced from my deathly coma like this several times during the first days after I was brought to the hospital.

"I was in such a bad way that it's a wonder Captain Jason bothered to have me patched up at all. For broken legs were not all that ailed me after the accident: on closer examination it turned out that I had been grazed on the hands and across the breast, a great wound gaped from my right eyelid to the nape of my neck. My diaphragm had burst when my lower intestines were thrust upward, putting so much pressure on my lungs that I had difficulty breathing, on top of which I had bruised five of my ribs. My right ankle had shattered, my foot was twisted back, and my thighbone had snapped at the ball joint on the left-hand side. This in turn had been stirred together in such a tangle that broken shards of bone had sliced through the muscle. The bones of my left hand had snapped, as had the fingers of my right. Both calves were also broken and split up to the knee joints; altogether, eleven bones were broken in twenty places. My left wrist and shoulder joints were sprained, and so were several other joints. And a large patch of my scalp had been flayed from my skull.

"Now I owed my life to the fact that Jason son of Aeson had been fostered and tutored by the centaur Cheiron, the greatest physician of his age. As there was a risk of my healing in a deformed posture, being so soft and mangled, he resorted to 'crucifying' me: nails were driven through both my legs and straps were tied to them, then belayed around two blocks on a pole at the end of the bed, and Jason tied a heavy sandbag to the end of each strap. Next, slings were placed under my knees, which were then hoisted up, each weighed down by a sandbag. It took me two weeks to get used to the 'cross' from which I was to hang for four months all together. All that time I suffered from a nagging ache in the nail holes, though this was alleviated when I drank the wine that Iphenoa brought me every morning.

"Before Jason could crucify me he had to bore holes through my legs below the knees, using a fairly hefty drill for the job. Apparently I told Jason that it would prove hard to drill through the bones of a man who had been granted the gift by blue-haired Poseidon of being impervious to sharp weapons. This proved correct, for the drill got stuck for an age in the bone, and one handle after another snapped off, but Jason broke through in the end and immediately started on the other leg.

"But it was not only the toughness of my legs that betrayed my past. During the struggle to heal myself my body reverted to the shape it used to have before my metamorphosis sixteen years earlier. I myself wasn't aware of this until one of the girls who helped me to breathe held up a mirror below my belly. I saw that my penis had shrunk until it exactly resembled the penis of a five-year-old boy, both in size and behavior, and its proportion to a man's body was like what you would see on a Renaissance sculpture (at last I understood why the nurses had been giggling at me). Moreover I had molted like a wolf in spring. My chest was white and soft again—with the swell of maidenly breasts.

"Yes, once I was a girl. My name was Caenis and I did as I pleased. We lived in Thessaly. My father, Elatus, was king of the Lapiths. He was a conventional man and the day I reached marriageable age he began to pester me to wed. It would certainly have been an easy task for the king to find me an eligible bridegroom—such as a hero who was both heir to a kingdom and a monster-slayer to boot—for I was famed throughout the lands for my intellect and radiant beauty. Indeed, I was so intelligent and fair that my half-brother Polyphemus used to call me Thena or Dite in an attempt to get a rise out of me. But as is often the case with independent girls, I paid little heed to my father's talk of marriage: like the grass that bears hermaphroditic flowers and fertilizes itself, I bloomed for myself alone.

"King Elatus found the situation most unfortunate, and the same could be said of the suitors who had waited full of anticipation for the day when the princess would be offered up for grabs. The greatest champions on Earth had gathered there, bold men and true; I would get to know many of them in my new life as a man, since several were destined to be my shipmates on the *Argo*.

"I was allowed to have my own way. The host of heroes moved on to the next country and commenced wooing the king's daughter there. My father turned to more agreeable tasks than bickering with his daughter. And who knows, my existence might have continued in this satisfactory state had news of the obdurate girl in Thessaly not carried beyond our mortal world.

"Not far from the city I had a secret refuge, a small

cove that I liked to visit at the kindling of the morning star. At that hour there was nothing more translucent under heaven than the shallow sea between the rocks. The seabed was everywhere visible and the water, blue as an eye, grew lighter the closer you got to the surface, until it turned green, then vanished—and I breathed it in.

"It was there that the god found me.

"The cove emptied of seawater. It was as if a wet quilt had been stripped from the ocean floor. There's a pretty shell, I thought to myself, and I walked over to a sugar-pink snail's house that lay on the sand. I bent down, picked up the conch, and weighed it in my hand: well, I never, here's a gift for Eurydice.

"Then the heavy wave broke over me.

"The surf raged in Poseidon's deep, cold eyes as he flung me flat on my back and crushed me beneath his weight. I tried to scream for help but he forced my teeth apart with his blue fingers and spat a mouthful of raw wet seaweed inside. I tried to wriggle out from beneath him but at the slightest movement my flesh and skin were lacerated by the coral that covered his thighs, the barnacles that grew on his palms; it was better to lie still while the god labored away on top of me, the shark oil oozing from his hair into my eyes. He did not cease until all the air had been knocked from my maidenly lungs and my veins were emptied of blood: then with a spasm of his hips he filled my body with seawater—his climactic groan echoed with the despairing cries of a thousand drowning men.

"The briny sea flooded every inch of my body: my belly and heart, my joints and limbs, every sinew, every muscle, every lymph node and nerve—and wherever it went it felt like molten iron poured into the outstretched hand of a child.

"Poseidon was well satisfied with his rut, and in return for my maidenhead he offered me one wish. I curled up where I lay on the shore and whimpered:

" 'I wish I were a man so I need never again endure such an ordeal.'

"These last words emerged in a deep masculine timbre, for the god had been as good as his word. And now that I was a man, Poseidon was generous to me, saying that from this time forth my nature would be such that no metal could harm me. He must have foreseen that I would have to take part in many a duel to defend my honor against men and giants who doubted my prowess because I had once been a maid.

"In my male shape I was given the name of Caeneus, and I remained in that form until the day war broke out between the Lapiths and the centaurs, which was when the latter drank themselves into a frenzy at the wedding of Pirithous and Hippodamia. A great battle was fought that you can read about in many books, for it was considered one of the mightiest clashes of antiquity. When the centaurs had given up trying to shoot me with javelins and arrows or run me through with swords and knives—and I had managed to kill their leader, Latreus—they resorted to bombarding me with rocks and huge tree trunks. I don't know whether tales of how badly I had been injured on Lemnos gave them this idea, but they piled so much of the forest on top of me that I was forced to change shape or perish.

"Long afterward the poet Naso quoted my brother-in-arms and former shipmate on the *Argo*, the seer Mopsus, as saying that a dun-colored bird had flown up from the pile and soared high into the sky in a wide circle above the battlefield. There it mewed sorrowfully before flying away.

"It was a young herring gull that had not yet acquired its adult plumage.

"It was I, Caeneus."

X

It was nearly one in the morning on Easter Day when Caeneus broke off his story so that someone could comfort the purser's lady friend, who had burst into tears when he described the rape of Caenis. At first she had borne up bravely, clamping her hand hard over her mouth and gesturing to the mate not to worry about her but to carry on, she would get over it. But when he said, "It was I, Caeneus," a paroxysm of sobbing escaped from behind her hand and she wailed:

"Oh, I can't bear it!"

The purser clasped an arm tightly around his lady friend's shoulders. She buried her face in his chest and wept there awhile. He stroked her hair gently, crooning something consoling, humming so deep in his chest that the melody vibrated low against her ear. The ensuing quiet gave me a chance to observe my dining companions' reactions to this heartwarming spectacle:

One word was written on all their faces:

"DEFEAT!"

Indeed, though the tune was meant for the purser's

lady friend alone, the song and the weeping were for all of us. Four years had passed since the end of the great conflict but we still couldn't believe that humanity had won.

The woman straightened up in her chair. She dried her eyes with her napkin, blew her nose, took a large gulp of water, and said:

"Right, I've had my cry."

The atmosphere relaxed a little and I got the impression that it was not the first time this had happened. The captain refilled our glasses. I drew attention to the lateness of the hour, which gave rise to a murmur of comment, but in spite of this Caeneus carried on from where he had left off:

"As the first child's cry sounded over Lemnos, I recovered my former physical strength and virility. But the Argonauts' conditions had deteriorated so greatly during their stay in the realm of doe-eyed Hypsipyle that it didn't seem wise to set me to work straightaway. Instead I was quartered with Heracles aboard the *Argo* for our last three weeks on Lemnos. Nevertheless, I had achieved more than might be expected of a badly injured man: Iphenoa was more than five months pregnant, and nine of the girls who had nursed me were with child by the time I was discharged from the hospital.

"Meanwhile, my crewmates' lot during those spring days was such that even as the babies began to be born in the palace, they were finishing their duties toward the women in the paupers' district and all that remained was to bed those who lived in She-wolf Alley; mostly prostitutes whom the queen had ordered to give up their trade—though the men did not find them particularly compliant. This combination of births and diminished living standards now finally had a dampening effect on the men's ardor, and many became frequent visitors to Heracles and his lads, who had by now been guarding the ship for nearly ten weary months.

"The visitors complained of their lot, moaning that they were kept constantly dashing from one end of town to the other, either flattening the straw with their verminous mistresses or lulling their infants to sleep in the palace apartments. And to crown it all, the mothers of their children were eager to start all over again.

"A lesser man than Heracles might have made use of this discontent to foment a mutiny against Jason son of Aeson. He would have summoned the men to him by night, hoisted the canvas, and sailed away, leaving the captain behind in the clutches of this strange nation of women. Instead he summoned Jason and they met by the side of the ship, at the crack of dawn, while I lay in my berth inside and overheard the whole thing.

"It was the spring equinox.

"I heard Heracles say:

"'Tell me one thing, brother: Who are the Argonauts? Are we hunted killers? Were we exiled from our lands for sacrilege or incest—forced to roam the seas like pirates? Why have we sat here so long, blockaded by women, going nowhere? Was it not our mission to achieve an impossible task? To triumph over monsters and witchcraft? To sail to the ends of the Earth and return with a priceless treasure?

"'Or do you intend your men to die of old age in the laundries of Lemnos, kneading the shit from the diapers of their baseborn offspring?'

"In that instant the spell seemed to lift from Captain Jason son of Aeson. He embraced Heracles, declaring that he had spoken well and justly, then ordered the crew to bid farewell to their mistresses and prepare the *Argo* for departure. He himself lay with Hypsipyle for the very last time, having by then begotten one son, Thoas, with her, and their lovemaking proved so potent that it resulted in another son, Euneus, who later became famous for providing the drink at the siege of Troy.

"The *Argo* weighed anchor.

"The wind was in our favor."

•

In the momentary silence that followed Caeneus's last words, I seized the chance, before people started clapping, to strike my wineglass with a teaspoon, then, rising to my feet, I announced:

"My dear shipmates! I must be permitted to say a few words. I wish to express my gratitude.

"We have been on this voyage now for seven days and

nights, soon to be eight, and it must be said that I have looked forward to every day. Throughout the voyage you have gone to great lengths to make my stay as agreeable as possible; Captain Alfredson has allotted me a regular seat at his table, the radiator in my cabin breaks down and before I can say 'Jack Robinson' someone has repaired it; I am invited on one motor excursion after another; there is always hot coffee in the pot when I come in from my turns about the deck; the steward has ironed my shirts. And although at times discord has raised its head between us 'supernumeraries,' it has always been resolved in the end. We are adults and know that it takes two to make a quarrel.

"Here in the saloon the atmosphere has invariably been homely; we have had music and dancing, and Mate Caeneus has entertained us with his life story—fascinating stuff for the most part, if a little on the racy side. But you are young; after the war we awoke to a new world—and the words of Dr. Pázmány, who predicted in 1927 that in the future sexual matters would be openly discussed at the dinner table, have been proved correct. Yes, high or low, young or old, you have shown me perfect amiability and respect.

"And this evening you have humored me yet again by having seafood for dinner; prawns and ocean clams with a creamy dill sauce on toast to begin, and poached salmon with potato gratin and melted butter for the main course. And although it was canned, not fresh, I have no complaints. I feel as if my Nordic temperament has been revitalized by this excellent and intelligently concocted repast. Little did I suspect that the seeds of the ideas I sowed in your minds with my points about 'fish and culture' would find here such fertile soil, would so soon bear such excellent fruit.

"I thank you for that!"

Raising my glass, I looked over the brim at each of my table companions in turn. I took a sip. I raised my glass anew. Lowering it, I did not replace it on the table but allowed it to remain in my hand. And for the rest of the speech I brandished the glass to emphasize my words:

"As I have lain in my cabin reflecting on your kindness to me, I have indulged myself in the belief that it has not been from obedience to your master alone but that perhaps you have derived some small pleasure from this old man's company on the voyage, just as he has unquestionably enjoyed yours.

"But now the adventure is over, tomorrow our ways must part. For, you see, I have decided to abandon ship and head for home . . ."

I paused to let the news sink in. They looked at one another in surprise, shaking their heads and exchanging comments in low voices. I raised my hand for silence, then carried on in the same friendly tone:

"One moment, please, one moment! In my letter of thanks to Mr. Magnus Jung-Olsen I will give you all the highest recommendation. It is nobody's 'fault,' merely that I feel I have already seen so many things, experienced so much, that I doubt the journey to Poti in Georgia could add anything new. But if anything interesting should happen on the voyage I do hope that when we meet again you will tell me the story—I will give Captain Alfredson my address and telephone number before I go.

"Finally, I would ask you all to be upstanding and drink a toast to the Jung-Olsen family and the Kronos shipping line."

Everyone rose to their feet and I led the toast:

"Long live the Jung-Olsen family and the Kronos line. Hip, hip, hurrah!"

•

When I returned to my quarters the fore cabin had been converted into a larder. From the way everything was arranged you would have thought it had been like that for the duration. It was a mystery to me how the purser and his lady friend had achieved this transformation without my being aware: the walls were lined with shelves, and through the wire netting—designed to keep everything in its place in heavy seas—I saw piles of tins, jars of pickled vegetables, and packets of flour, sugar, and spice. There were sacks of potatoes in one corner, and a stack of boxes of wine and fruit juice by the door, all lashed down with leather straps. In the middle of the cabin stood a huge refrigerator.

My luggage, however, was nowhere to be seen.

My first reaction was to assume that this was a practical joke in honor of my departure, something typical of life at sea and traditionally performed the night before men left the ship. But I soon realized that this couldn't be right as I hadn't told anyone I was leaving until just now. It must be some kind of misunderstanding. I was about to return to the saloon to ask Alfredson what was going on when the memory of the send-off I had just received prevented me; it had been so heartwarming:

The men had hugged me. The purser's lady friend wished me bon voyage on the long journey that lay before me as I returned home to Copenhagen overland. Mate Caeneus had laid his great fist on my shoulder and said: "Goodbye for now, brother Valdimar." And I invited him to drop the formality.

No, there was no need to spoil this happy memory by carping about something that must have a perfectly rational explanation.

I decided to investigate the matter a little further and opened the door to the bathroom. It was dark and the light switch wouldn't work, but once my eyes had grown accustomed to the gloom I saw that here, too, someone had been busy. Bath and shower, mirror and basin, bench and cupboard had all gone and instead of white tiles the floor was now covered with black earth. The blood froze in my veins. For a split second I thought I saw the huge figure of a man standing where the shower used to be.

Then the moon crept out from behind a cloud and shone in through the porthole—and its rays revealed a suit of armor hanging on a purpose-built stand; on top was a burnished bronze helmet with a high, billowing feather crest; beneath it gleamed the breastplate, molded for a muscular giant, while down on the floor stood a pair of greaves, showing what strong legs the owner must have.

I was standing in an armory. There were rows of halberds and daggers, bows and quivers, maces and axes, spears and swords. Beside the armor stood a shield the size of a wagon wheel, propped up against the wall so that it gleamed in the moonlight. An etching in flaming silver screamed from the center of the shield; the head of the Gorgon with her swine's tushes, venomous eyes, and hissing snakes.

I fled out of the bathroom, through the fore cabin and into the saloon, slamming the door behind me. Yes, there was no mistaking it, this was the door to the quarters I'd had the use of for the last seven days and nights; no other fitted the description. I looked from the cabin door over to the captain's table. There was no one there. I shouted his name:

"Captain Alfredson, Captain Alfredson!"

No answer. I hurried across the empty saloon and looked to see if there was anyone in the galley. No one there. I stuck my head into the lounge, the radio room, the bridge. I went along the deckhands' corridor, banging on all the doors: I knocked on the doors of both mates, of the engineers, of Alfredson himself. But there was not a soul to be seen anywhere. This was quite an ordeal for an elderly man and I frequently had to stop and catch my breath.

It was not until my third circuit of the ship that I noticed the door down to the engine room was open a crack. It hadn't occurred to me to go down there as I was wearing my best suit, which I was unwilling to dirty since it looked as if it would be my only outfit for the homeward journey.

I opened the door and called:

"Hello! Is there anybody there?"

No answer.

I was no more than halfway down the companion-way when I saw that the whole crew was assembled there, including the purser's lady friend. They were all dressed in white coats and stood around a black platform in the middle of the engine room. The platform was about four feet high and at a guess twenty-four feet in diameter. An imposing four-sided prism jutted up from the center, revolving with infinite slowness, while from inside the platform came a heavy ticking, a slow, deep pulse. This was the only sound that could be described as an engine noise—there was nothing else resembling an engine to be seen.

Next I heard the sound of effortful groans and the onlookers stepped aside for the first engineer, who came walking backward, guiding four deckhands who struggled over to the platform under the weight of a man-high key for winding a clock, all of them clad in white coats. Here they dispersed, one climbing onto the platform to receive the key, the other three lifting it. Then these three climbed onto the platform too, and together the four of them lugged the key to the prism. The engineer signaled to them to hoist the key, and they held it suspended over the prism while the engineer guided it into place, then they lowered it. The engineer and deckhands jumped down from the platform. The captain nodded:

"Good work, lads . . ."

At this point Caeneus appeared. He took up position by the platform and the purser's lady friend helped him out of his white coat. Caeneus was now wearing nothing but a loincloth. He stepped up onto the platform, walked once counterclockwise around the key, then stopped and flexed his muscles like a wrestler. He stroked quickly but firmly over his biceps and thighs, spat on his palms, then set to work on the key.

As the second mate turned the key in a clockwise direction, his pliant body gleamed in the dim light of the engine room.

I yelled:

"What about my cabin?"

Captain Alfredson was the only one who looked around. He seemed to have been expecting me and called back:

"Don't be alarmed, Mr. Haraldsson, everything will be fine."

He turned to the ship's steward and jerked his thumb over his shoulder at me:

"Make up a bed for him in Caeneus's cabin . . ."

And he added so that everyone could hear:

"The old man can sleep there tonight. It'll take Caeneus till noon to wind up the ship . . ."

HOMECOMING

XI

My neighbors say I have changed since I came home from my voyage. And I respond with the following question:

"What is the point of traveling if not to broaden your mind?"

They like this answer and we chat a little about our travels, past and present, for most of us who live here are getting on in years. One sign that I am an altered man is that I have changed the topic of my conversation at Café Sommerfugl. I haven't entirely given up discussing the influence of seafood on the Nordic race but I spend less time discoursing on this and more on the fittings on board the MS *Elizabet Jung-Olsen*. Everyone is amazed at how well I was treated. "Is that right?" and "You don't say!" are the most common reactions to my tales, and I am often asked to describe my quarters or explain certain events in more detail. In particular, they are interested in the fact that I witnessed a possible crime, and I have often been called on to repeat the story of my dealings with Chief Officer Knud Hamsun.

Sometimes a disgruntled voice will pipe up:

"I wouldn't have believed it if I hadn't it heard with my own ears that a fascist like Magnus Jung-Olsen had it in his stinking bones to be kind to an old addlepate like you . . ."

But only one man speaks like that; the owner of Café Sommerfugl. He lost an ear in a German penal camp and has been bitter ever since; he can't bear people to talk about anything other than that ear of his. We discussed it for the first year and a half after he came home—and from time to time after that—but have long since tired of this topic. When he starts on his ear, we regulars say:

"Everyone prefers what's there to what's not."

Another thing that has changed is my attitude to Widow Lauritzen. Before I went on my travels I thought her foolish and tiresome, and neglectful of her garden. I am still of the opinion that she could take better care of her apple trees and currant bushes, and I am not alone in that. She is the only one of us who has the chance to do any gardening, since the other apartments do not come with plots of their own. But I don't find her tiresome anymore.

Shortly after my return to Copenhagen, the lady turned to me in the line at the fishmonger's and said archly:

"Oh, so the Viking has returned?"

For everyone here knows that I am an Icelander.

> The waves and the hull were clashing,
> the surf on the rails was splashing,

the winds in the sails were lashing;
the ocean my ship was smashing.

I recited by way of reply. She laughed, saying she always loved hearing Icelandic spoken even though she couldn't understand a word. And one thing led to another until we had become the best of friends.

Now we dine together twice a week, on Tuesdays and Fridays, and the meal is held at my apartment because I like to be host. We contribute to the spread jointly, and if Madame Lauritzen wishes to eat meat I have decided not to object. She brings it herself, as her grandson is a butcher and often slips nice treats to his grandmother, while I have a herring salad or buy myself a deep-fried plaice from the sandwich shop in the next street. In this manner we avoid conflict and the evening passes in cozy chat about life and everything.

The widow is well informed about all kinds of current affairs, as her husband was some sort of poet, so she can tell me news from the world of theater, music, and literature. She does this in her frank and cheerful manner, and her accounts are always diverting, though the subject matter is undeniably often lightweight. I myself speak of international affairs and the most topical issues in contemporary science, chiefly dietetics, the importance of which has greatly increased as a result of all the reconstruction following the war.

I have mentioned before that I live in an apartment

consisting of two rooms, one of which performs a three-fold role as kitchen, dining room, and sitting room, with a bedroom opening off it (I share a lavatory with others on my floor and the showers are in the basement). When the widow comes for dinner I leave the bedroom door ajar and turn the kitchen table sideways so that one or other of us has a view inside.

We make it a rule that if Madame Lauritzen is "not in the mood" she will sit in the chair nearer the kitchen while I sit with my back to the bedroom door, but when she is "in the mood" she sits on the bedroom side and I sit facing her. From there I can see both the lady and the door half open behind her and beyond it the bed that awaits us. So we need never discuss whether the lady is "in the mood" or not. I, on the other hand, am always "in the mood," and this is the most significant change that has taken place in me since the voyage with Captain Alfredson and his crew.

I have placed a decent desk under the bedroom window and spend my days sitting on the edge of my bed, writing these memoirs or else articles for fishing periodicals in Iceland. On the top right-hand corner of the desk there is a small bundle that at first sight might appear to be nothing more than a folded napkin from the Kronos shipping line. The company's logo is embroidered on it in wine-red thread:

A winged hourglass hovers over the sea with two

crossed sledgehammers beneath, both pointing to the right.

But inside this innocent-looking napkin I keep the object that, with its odor and unusual properties, has reinvigorated my potency in the sexual arena. Yes, the night I stayed in Caeneus's cabin I discovered the splinter from the bowsprit of the *Argo* in the inside pocket of his officer's jacket, which was hanging over the back of a chair. And I spirited it away with me when I left the MS *Elizabet Jung-Olsen* on Easter morning last spring. It was some compensation for my luggage, which never turned up.

Yesterday evening when I took out the splinter of the *Argo* and began to toy with it, as I always do before burrowing under the bedclothes with Widow Lauritzen, there was a tap on the bedroom window. We were both startled, as I live on the third floor; the drainpipe is next to the sitting-room window, and it is unthinkable that any human being could climb so high. There was another tap, louder than the first. I drew back the curtains.

A herring gull was perched on the sill outside. It struck its yellow beak against the windowpane, flapped its wings, and squawked:

"ARRK! ARRK!"

To the lady's great amusement I mimicked it:

"ARRK! ARRK!"

And drew the curtains again.

SOURCES

Sources used in the writing of *The Whispering Muse*:

Argonautica by Apollonius of Rhodes
Medea by Euripides
Hypsipyle by Euripides
Innan lands og utan (Home and Abroad) by Matthías
 Thórdarson frá Móum
Fiskneysla og menning (Fish Consumption and Culture)
 by Matthías Thórdarson frá Móum
Ég sigli minn sjó (Life on the Ocean Wave), the memoirs
 of Hrafn Valdimarsson
Enn sigli ég sjóinn (More Life on the Ocean Wave), the
 memoirs of Hrafn Valdimarsson
Metamorphoses by Ovid
Trójumannasaga in forna (The Ancient Saga of the Men
 of Troy)